W9-BGN-496

Rookie
Quarterback

Other Books by Jackson Scholz

———

Batter Up
Fielder from Nowhere
The Football Rebels

Rookie
Quarterback

JACKSON SCHOLZ

Morrow Junior Books
New York

Z/328

Copyright © 1965 by Jackson Scholz. Reissued by both Morrow Junior Books and
Beech Tree Books in 1993
with changes that update the text for contemporary readers.

Book Design by Logo Studios/B. Gold
Printed in the United States of America.

1 2 3 4 5 6 7 8 9 10

Library of Congress Cataloging-in-Publication Data
Scholz, Jackson Volney.   Rookie quarterback / by Jackson Scholz.   p.   cm.
Summary: A high-school dropout returns from the Navy, revives his
dedication to football, and is inspired to secure his future by
using his academic as well as athletic abilities.
ISBN 0-688-12524-7.
[1. Football—Fiction.]   I. Title.
PZ7.S37Ro   1993   [Fic]—dc20   92-43375   CIP   AC

Publisher's Note

Football is played much differently today than it was in the 1960's. There have been alterations in equipment and safety standards, but the most significant changes have resulted from new substitution rules. Traditional substitution rules reflected football's origins in rugby and stated that a player who left the game in one quarter could not return until the following quarter. This led most team members to play on both offense and defense; many would play an entire game without once leaving the field. These early players were therefore skilled at many positions, and a star player, like Clint Martin in *The Football Rebels* (another Scholz novel from this same period), might have been the first-string quarterback, safety, punter, placekicker, and kick returner. The incredible conditioning required to play sixty continuous minutes of football on both sides of the line of scrimmage earned these players the nickname "ironmen."

Fielding a team of eleven "ironmen" demanded an offense constructed around their basic all-around abilities. Early football teams used a simple offensive strategy— running the ball almost exclusively and passing only when necessary. For the power and versatility this strategy required, there was no better offensive weapon than the T-formation. In this configuration, the quarterback lined up directly behind the center, with the fullback several yards behind him. Two halfbacks flanked the fullback, forming a "T" in the backfield. The left and right ends were positioned on the line and, although eligible for pass receptions, were used primarily as blockers. By placing this many players close to the ball, the "T" enabled teams to block powerfully and produce consistent running gains. On a given play, the quarterback could hand the ball off to any of his three runningbacks, run with it himself, or throw a pass to one of the two ends for a quick completion. This play-calling flexibility kept defenses guessing while still providing the offensive punch necessary to win football games.

Soon after World War II, professional football changed its rules to allow unlimited substitutions. This policy was instituted to accomodate the sudden flood of talented young war veterans who were now eager to make their mark on the professional gridiron. As coaches became accustomed to these new substitution rules, they realized that they could develop specialty players who were excellent at just one position rather than moderately skilled in several. Defensive coordinators sought huge but slow defensive linemen to stop the T-formation offense in its tracks. Offensive coordinators responded with light, fast receivers and quarterbacks with powerful arms to get the ball to them. Touchdowns could be scored quickly and consistently, and coaches scrambled to accomodate this new passing attack. The slow moving, tightly packed T-formation was soon made obsolete by intricate pass-oriented formations with more eligible receivers on the line and fewer runningbacks in the backfield. Catching the fever of this exciting brand of football, college and semi-professional leagues followed suit and changed their substitution rules in the mid-1960's.

Nowadays, the only place to see the T-formation is in high school and college football, where the teams have neither the practice time nor the skilled players to develop complex offensive schemes. The simplicity and power of the T-formation and its modern variation, the wishbone, still give these games the grinding "fourth-down-and-inches-to-go" excitement of old-time football that Jackson Scholz has captured and immortalized in his football novels *Rookie Quarterback* and *The Football Rebels*.

Rookie
Quarterback

Chapter One

It was a fine September afternoon, with the hint of crispness that caused football fans to sniff the breeze and know the time was near. Tim Barlow's clouded eyes and melancholy air contrasted sharply with the weather.

He had not planned to attend this early practice session of the Greytown Cougars. In fact, he had not planned to attend any Cougar practice sessions, but his resolve failed him. So here he was, moving grudgingly toward a situation that was bound to recall painful moments. Yet, as he approached the action on the field, a slow excitement quivered through his nerves. He wondered briefly why sandlot football should excite him; then in another surge of honesty he knew that any football could excite him.

Tim joined the group of spectators near the side line,

hoping to remain unnoticed. He watched the early season scrimmage critically, noting with surprise that it was well-coordinated and effective, hardly the style of football expected from a sandlot team made up of a strange assortment of players, ranging from kids just out of high school to mature, successful businessmen.

They were having fun, no doubt about it, yet underneath Tim sensed a serious dedication to the game, an attitude he could easily understand. These men loved football. They retained the urge to play, and sandlot football was the outlet to their energy. They collected lumps and bruises with no hope of glory as compensation.

The Cougars, as opposed to many sandlot teams, were well-uniformed and organized, a tribute to the football buffs of Greytown, who backed their enthusiasm with hard cash. The gridiron was laid out on the local baseball field. Its bleachers could not hold the crowds that came to watch the Cougar games.

The Cougars' greatest asset was their coach, Bart Hogan, a bear of a man who had been a great defensive lineman for the big-league Mohawks. He was Greytown's leading lawyer, and if Hogan's clients did not receive his full attention during football season, it was their hard luck. As a coach, Bart Hogan had the gift many former football players lack: he knew the game and could impart his knowledge to the men he worked with. The Cougars, in their league, were formidable.

Tim Barlow moved along the side line, following the play and deliberately leaving the other fans, some of whom had begun to recognize him. He feared that the curious attention might be followed up with questions. Luckily, none of his old acquaintances were among the fans. He'd been a fool to come.

He was about to leave to avoid further risk when Hogan passed him. The coach glanced casually in Tim's direction, took a few more strides, then whirled swiftly for a double take.

"Hey!" said Hogan. "You're Tim Barlow!"

There was something slightly comical about Hogan's pleased surprise. It forced a grin from Hogan. "Am I?" he inquired.

"You'd better be," said Hogan. "I need a quarterback."

"I'm afraid you'll have to keep on looking."

Hogan eyed Tim shrewdly for a moment, sensing the lack of conviction of Tim's tone. "These boys are about ready for their showers. Wait for me. We'll talk."

Hogan's courtroom tactics were effective. He turned and walked away as if the matter were settled. Tim did not want to wait nor did he want to talk, but Hogan had beaten him to the punch. Leaving now would be downright rude.

So Tim waited. Hogan indicated that the talk would not be hurried when he led the way to the bleachers and settled himself on the lower tier. He stretched his legs in front of him, leaning back to rest his elbows on the second row of seats. Without words, he managed to create an atmosphere of relaxation intended to set the tone of his interview with Tim. Tim had no choice but to take a seat beside the older man.

Hogan said, "I haven't seen you around since you left high school."

"You probably mean," corrected Tim, "since I dropped out of high school."

Hogan slowly turned his head toward Tim. "I usually say what I mean, son," he reproved. "Also, if I had used the term dropout I wouldn't have made it sound like a dirty word."

"Everybody else makes it sound that way."

After a moment of silence, Hogan said, "None of this is any of my business, Tim. I'll confess a personal interest in you as a football player, but beyond that it's a matter of sheer curiosity. How does a situation of this sort come about? You were one of the finest high school football players I've ever seen, and I've seen a lot. You had a great future as a quarterback. Then you dropped out of high school and served two years in the Navy. I'd like to know how it happened—if you'd care to talk about it."

Tim found to his amazement that he did want to talk about it. The problem had been bottled up inside him too long, building a pressure that was becoming dangerous.

He let his breath out slowly, "Okay, where shall I begin?"

"Why not at the beginning—if there is one?"

"Yes, I guess there is. I had a bout with polio when I was four. I weathered it all right, but naturally it slowed me down a lot."

"You were lucky to come out of it without permanent damage."

"Mighty lucky. When I was able to start school, though, I was two years behind my class. I never made it up, so I was always older and bigger than any other boy in my class. You know how kids are—most of them looked on me as a big awkward dummy, a sort of freak. It wasn't very pleasant."

"I don't imagine it was."

"By the time I got to high school my muscles were beginning to catch up with my size. My coordination improved and I began to move with more confidence. In the summer after my freshman year I developed so fast it almost seemed to happen overnight. I'd always wanted to play football, but was too clumsy. It wasn't like that anymore. I played that fall and—well, I must have had a knack for it."

"An understatement," Hogan said.

"Football," Tim went on, "was all that mattered to me. Suddenly I was a big shot, a really important guy instead of an overgrown stumblebum, and the change came so fast I couldn't take it in my stride. My head swelled up like a balloon. And that was that."

Tim checked the narrative, aware that he might sound long-winded.

"So you eased up on your classwork," Hogan prompted in a way that left no doubt he was deeply interested.

"I practically ignored it," Tim continued, grateful for the chance to get everything off his chest. "I barely squeezed past my sophomore year, and in my junior year I flunked just about everything but math, which happens to come easy to me. In the meanwhile, we had two un-defeated seasons, and everybody gave me most of the credit."

"Which you deserved," said Hogan flatly. "So what happened next?"

"*You* know what happened next," said Tim impatiently.

"I'd like to hear your version."

Tim shrugged. "Okay. When I had to repeat my junior year, I became ineligible for football, and I was about as popular around school as a case of smallpox. I was a first-class jerk for crippling the football team. I was a lousy traitor to the school, and no one let me forget it. I swallowed it for a while, then couldn't take it any longer. While I was still sore and blaming everyone and everything but myself, I joined the Navy for a two-year hitch. I got out a couple of days ago."

"Have you got a job?"

"Not yet. Besides, who wants a highschool dropout for anything but his strong back?"

"Plenty of successful men never got as far as high school," Hogan said.

"I know it. But those men knew where they were going. I don't."

"Maybe if you played a little football with the Cougars you'd get a different slant on things," suggested Hogan.

Tim shook his head. "The whole mess started with football," he said grimly. "If I played again, what would it lead to?"

"You could finish high school and get a college football scholarship," Hogan said, unwilling to give up.

"Same deal," Tim answered stubbornly. "I'd probably flunk out of college too. I think I know myself pretty well by this time."

Hogan stared quizzically at Tim, then slowly shook his head as if admitting that his eloquence was of no avail. He finally said, "I honestly doubt that you know yourself at all. I've known a lot of mixed-up people, but you're the champ."

"Yes," said Tim without resentment, "I'm the champ."

Bart Hogan stood up, handling his weight with an ease that belied his middle age. He moved away, leaving Tim with a strong conviction that the Cougar coach had joined a lot of other people in their low regard for him. Tim rose to his feet too, feeling bitter and resentful—a familiar feeling these days.

He watched Hogan walk toward the Cougars' limited supply of footballs lying on the ground awaiting safe storage for the night. Hogan glanced across his shoulder, then stooped to pick up one of the balls. His next move was sudden and unexpected. He turned, his arm snapped back, and the ball came flashing toward Tim Barlow like a brown projectile.

Tim's reaction was purely automatic, a swift reflex. Yet the long-neglected move was accurate and exactly timed. His big hands met the ball and reduced its speed with shock-absorbing ease. He held it for a moment near his face, savoring the sensations he had missed for several years, the almost painful pleasure of touching a football's smooth hard surface and smelling the odor of fine leather.

He fondled the football for another moment before accusing Hogan hoarsely. "That was a dirty trick."

"I'm the sneaky type," confessed Hogan. "Throw it back."

Tim curled his hand around the ball. His fingertips, by instinct, found the lacing welt. He threw the ball in a smooth, clear arc, happily surprised that it maintained its steady flight and scored a bull's-eye. Hogan and Tim passed the ball back and forth in silence. Hogan threw off-target several times, testing Tim's getaway speed and the sureness of his hands. The coach was pleased with what he saw.

He asked finally, "What's your weight?"

"Two fifteen."

"Any fat?"

"The Navy doesn't leave fat on its sailors."

Bart Hogan held the ball and walked toward Tim. "Have you changed your mind?" he demanded bluntly.

"Yes, I've changed it," Tim said grudgingly. "You win."

"Tomorrow at four-thirty," Hogan said.

"I'll be here," promised Tim.

Chapter Two

Tim was frightened by the ease with which he'd made the decision to play football. The history of his impulsive moves was bad enough to leave him little confidence in snap judgments. He had come to regard them as a sign of weakness, as a tendency to run in the opposite direction when the going got too hot.

At the age of twenty-two he had little to look back on with pride. At a time when most men had started a career, he found himself still floundering in a world that seemed to jeer, "You had your chance, son, and you bungled it." Tim recognized that he was wasting too much time feeling sorry for himself, and that he often imagined the people of Greytown were looking down their noses at him. They had other things to think about, things more important than the problems of a high-school dropout whom they hadn't seen for two years.

True, Tim's mother and father had been badly disappointed when he failed to finish high school, but now that he was home again he had no cause to doubt their love. No mention had been made as yet of Tim's future business plans, which was just as well, because he had none.

He intended, of course, to find a job as soon as he became accustomed once more to civilian life. He had saved enough money while in the Navy to indulge himself in this respect. His father owned a small, modestly profitable hardware store, but Tim had no intention of asking his father to make a place for him. There was room only for the old employee who had been with his father for many years. Tim decided, therefore, to join the Cougars for a while, hoping, as Bart Hogan had suggested, that a little active football might help him adjust.

Tim reported for practice with a few misgivings. He could not be entirely sure that the football talent he had shown in high school had survived his long absence from the game. It seemed unlikely that his skill would be gone, but the possibility was there, and he would not know for sure until the action started. He was certain, though, that the game still held tremendous fascination for him and that his desire to play was still intense and intact. That desire in itself, he reasoned, was a vital asset.

His next concern was acceptance by the other members of the team. It stood to reason that they should be glad to welcome a strong player, but he never could tell about people. Tim assumed that the squad was a closely

knit unit of local men with fierce pride in their achievements on the gridiron. Perhaps they might resent the
invasion of an outsider, a term that Tim felt applied to him.
Another touchy situation might arise if the present quarterback lost his job to Tim as Hogan had intimated he
would.

None of the players had arrived when Tim got to the
field at four-thirty. Most of them were men who could not
leave their jobs until five o'clock, and who then hurried to
join the team for the pleasure of being battered about for
two delightful hours under the driving force of their law-
yer-coach.

Hogan was on hand, however, with a football uniform for Tim. He led the way to the dressing room beneath the bleachers. It was of ample size, and snug with
electric heat for chilly weather and electric heating for the
showers.

"The boys live high," said Tim, surprised.

"Dave Grant, our right guard, is a building contrac-
tor," explained Hogan. "He brought a crew out here and
did the work at cost."

Tim's surprise increased when he unpacked his gear.
"This looks like good stuff," he said, examining a lightweight shoulder harness with skillfully suspended pads,
the first of its type he had ever seen. "These things cost
money."

"They do at that," said Hogan with a touch of smugness. "It's what I tell the town boys—nothing's too good for the Cougars."

"Do they do this voluntarily?"

"Most of them," said Hogan. Then, grinning, he added, "There are a few scrooges, of course, but they're usually eager to oblige after we've reasoned with them."

"I see," said Tim, tactfully abandoning the subject. Bart Hogan obviously had his own ways, legally unassailable and convincing, of persuading reluctant supporters of his beloved football team.

"I forgot to ask your shoe size," Hogan said, "so I brought several pairs along. One pair ought to fit you."

Tim found a perfect fit. When he started to put on his uniform, Hogan said, "You won't need pads today. I want to scrape some of the barnacles off you before starting contact work."

The Cougars began to arrive by the time Tim had finished dressing. He had anticipated a few awkward moments, but none materialized. The men, some in business clothes and some in working clothes, lost identity with anything but football the minute they stepped into the dressing room. Whatever their relations off the football field, here they were solidly bound by a common interest. They were football players, nothing more. They accepted Tim as a football player when they were introduced to him. Quite a few remembered him and seemed sincerely pleased to have him with the Cougars. Tim watched warily for some hint of disapproval of the way he had acted in the past and was able to relax when no one referred to it.

He relaxed even more when a husky man about his own age came up to him, and said, "I'm Ray Coburn and I want to present you with the keys to the quarterback spot. You're sure welcome to them."

"Well—well, thanks," said Tim uneasily. "But—"

"Don't thank *me*," said Coburn. "Bart seemed to think I was the best man for the job. I did what I could, but we both know the spot can be improved. Maybe if I'm a good boy he'll put me back at left end where I belong."

"I don't know whether I'll be an improvement," said Tim with a grin, "but I'll do the best I can."

The next few days were interesting for Tim, but not particularly exciting. Hogan's method of scraping off the barnacles consisted mostly of routines that concentrated on the fundamentals. Tim resented the drills at first, but he was quick to acknowledge that even a good high school coach, such as the one he had worked with, was not comparable to a man with professional football training.

Tim thought he knew how to tackle until a few sessions with the tackling dummy taught him otherwise. He had considered himself a fine passer until Bart Hogan smoothed out several wrinkles and improved Tim's accuracy and distance. When punting, Tim learned to get the ball away much faster and with more assurance than he ever had before. His respect for Hogan grew.

Tim's regard for him was not prompted entirely by his own improvement. Hogan handled the Cougars as a whole with remarkable skill. Tim understood that the coach was not dealing with a team cast in the usual high school or college mold. These men had achieved independence off the football field. They were not inspired to fight, fight, fight for the glory of their alma mater. They played football for just one reason—because they wanted to. Nevertheless, Bart Hogan's job was still to maintain their interest in the game, and he seemed to have a genius for it.

He was complete boss, no doubt about it, yet he tempered his authority with uncanny understanding of the players he worked with. He knew just how far to drive men who sat all day at desks, and he knew the fatigue threshold of men who toiled at manual labor. He fitted these facts together like a jigsaw puzzle and came up with an uncluttered picture. He also came up with men on his team who could face a buffalo stampede if Hogan asked them to.

Tim learned the Cougars' signals. By necessity, they were simple, yet Tim memorized them with a speed that raised Bart Hogan's eyebrows. He quizzed Tim rapidly, and Tim answered his questions without hesitation.

"Hmmm," mused Hogan.

"I've got a knack for numbers, signals, and formations," Tim explained. "As I said before, I'm pretty good at math."

"You must be," Hogan said. "The next thing is, can you pull those signals out of a hat at the right time during a game?"

"I don't know," Tim confessed.

"We'll soon find out. I'll let you scrimmage some tomorrow," promised Hogan. "And as soon as you and the boys get used to each other, I'll let you run one of the teams."

Scrimmage on the following day gave Tim no chance to demonstrate his leadership, even though it made several important contributions to his football education. The scrimmage was devoted largely to the perfection of some routine plays whose success depended on accurate blocking and close timing. Playing quarterback for the offensive squad, Tim found to his chagrin that he still had lots to learn about the swift, deceptive ball handling so essential in the T formation.

Hogan, though his standards were high, was a fine teacher, and Tim Barlow was a fine pupil. Tim learned fast. He accepted criticism without resentment and he soaked up instruction like a thirsty sponge. As Tim well knew, no two centers snap the ball the same way, and as soon as he became accustomed to big Tom Jurgen's firm, hard style, Tim could concentrate with more confidence on his pivots and his hand-offs. These moves, too, improved as soon as he had gauged the speed and ability of his backfield men. He was soon handing them the ball in the spot that seemed to suit them best rather than the one he might find more convenient for himself. Hogan began nodding with approval.

Tim learned another important lesson—the hard way. The Cougars had been divided into two balanced teams. Tim noted with approval that Hogan kept moving in fresh substitutes in order to give everyone a chance to play. Tim was also aware that the men were playing with a fierceness that hardly seemed in keeping with a practice session, and he assumed that the Cougars played like this *all* the time for the sheer pleasure of it.

When Hogan told the offensive team to run a keeper play, Tim's pulse took a couple of extra hops. Hogan was giving him the chance he had been waiting for, the chance to run with the ball. The defensive squad was not expecting the maneuver, and Tim intended to look good on this one.

The play got under way with smooth precision. Tim took the snap from center, made a quarter turn, and faked a hand-off to the fullback, who slanted his plunge off tackle on the left side of the line. The neat deception drew a couple of the defensive linebackers to the danger point. Tim hesitated just long enough to suggest he had completed his assignment, then, concealing the ball behind his hip, completed his turn and set off around the right side of the line.

The play looked good right from the start. Tim had

a pair of halfbacks out in front of him for blocking, and the defensive left end had been boxed out of action. One of the halfbacks had missed his assigned block, but Tim had gained enough speed to be out of danger. When he saw the safety man moving up fast to nail him near the side line, Tim cut in toward a tempting opening at the line of scrimmage.

It looked like a good opening, that is, until Tim saw an alert defensive back charge in to plug it. The man was a threat, of course, but Tim had weathered similar threats. He could see that the man would not arrive in time to be well balanced for a tackle, so it was merely a matter of swerving slightly before running past the man's wild grab. The same technique had worked in high school many times.

This time it did not work. Tim's miscalculation was of epic proportions. Instead of plowing through the fellow's outstretched arm, Tim felt as if someone had slammed him in the belly with a fence post. The arm bent slightly, but it did not give. Tim's breath came out in a mighty grunt, and when he hit the ground he was content to stay there for a while in rueful contemplation of the difference between the tackle of a strong man and that of a high school kid. He filed this bit of information carefully away.

Once assured that Tim had merely had the wind knocked out of him, Bart Hogan stood above him grinning. Tim's tackler, a young farmer named Bates, extended a hand to help him from the ground. Tim accepted it without hesitation. "Not quite the same as high school, huh?" said Hogan, still amused. "I wanted you to find it out."

"I found it out, and I'll remember it." Then, managing a grin of his own, he told Bates, "I'll also try to remember I'm playing with men instead of boys."

"In that case," Bates assured him, "it won't be so easy for me next time. I hope not anyway, because we're counting on you."

"Thanks," said Tim. "I'll do my best."

Chapter Three

In the following week Tim Barlow learned more football than he had ever learned in high school. He had known, of course, that there was lots to learn, yet it came as a surprise to find that he was ignorant of so many things that seemed vitally important once they had been brought to his attention.

To begin with, he was playing a rougher brand of football than he had ever played before. His natural running power, which had been so effective in high school, was far less effective against strong, well-coached men. Now the length of his runs depended on the skill with which he used his blockers and on the wisdom of the split-second decisions he was forced to make when the defense closed in on him.

Passing was another factor—a big one. His passing

had been a major threat against high school teams. Not only had he been able to throw the ball much better than the average high school quarterback, but pass defense, for the most part, had been loose and sloppy, permitting him ample time to pick up his receiver. It was different on this team. Bart Hogan made the most of his defensive backfield speed. A successful pass depended on a tight pass pattern, close timing, and, above all, pinpoint accuracy. To his own and Hogan's satisfaction, Tim improved each day.

His improvement was aided to a large extent by the right end, Nick Jeffer, a tall rangy man about Tim's age. Nick possessed an ambling, deceptive speed and a tricky change of pace that could usually get him to the right place at the right time and that often befuddled pass defenders. Best of all, Nick's glue-fingered hands could grab the ball out of the air when it looked as if he had no chance to catch it.

Tim confided to Bart Hogan, "You've taught me a lot about passing, but this guy, Nick Jeffer, makes me look better than I actually am. Where did you get hold of him?"

Hogan stared unbelievingly at Tim, then asked, "You don't know who he is?"

Tim admitted guiltily, "I guess I don't." Defending himself, he went on, "I—well, I've spent most of my time by myself lately, trying to figure what everything is all about. Who is he?"

"An all-American."

"What?"

"You could call him that at any rate. He wasn't first choice on all the teams, though personally I think he should have been. The all-American selection these days depends largely on publicity, and Nick went to a relatively small college. Nevertheless, he was high on the draft list and had several good pro offers."

"Why did he turn them down?"

"He decided to go into business with his father."

Tim was impressed. He had never had such close contact with an all-American, and he found it hard to subdue a feeling of awe toward a player of Nick's reputation.

The next day Hogan bore down hard on pass plays and pass defense, sending play after play through the air. He may have wanted to find out how Tim would react to what he had learned about Nick Jeffer. If so, Hogan found out plenty. Much too aware that he was heaving passes at an all-American, Tim tried hard to make each pass exactly perfect.

The results were sad, and Tim began to sweat with nervousness. He was waiting for Nick to show temper or disgust as he had every right to do. Finally, on an in-and-out pass play in which Tim was supposed to find his target near the side line, he was relieved to note that the pass was somewhat better than others he had thrown. Even so, it led the receiver a shade too much. Nick got his fingertips on the ball, juggled it for a moment, then let it get away from him. While the ball was still bobbling on the ground, Nick kicked it angrily into the end zone. It was the gesture of a man who had taken all he could.

Tim squirmed with apprehension while Nick stalked back toward the line of scrimmage. It seemed, to Tim at least, that a great football player was about to tell an unknown football player a few things about forward passing. Tim believed he deserved all he was about to get, but thought he might make things a little easier for himself by promptly admitting his guilt.

He took several steps toward the angry end, and then blurted, "I'm sorry, Nick. Those were lousy passes I've been shooting at you."

Nick stopped, stared at Tim in a puzzled way, then burst into laughter. Seeing the confusion on Tim's face, he hurried to explain, "I wasn't sore at *you*. I was sore at myself. I should have had that last one. I must be getting old and rusty."

"But—but it wasn't a good pass," Tim insisted.

"I've seen better ones," said Nick with a grin, "but look at it this way. These are practice sessions, and if you dropped them all right in my hands, I wouldn't have much practice. Just heave the ball in my general direction and let me do the worrying."

Tim's liking for Nick Jeffer took an upward swing. Nick had let him off the hook in an easy, natural way instead of making an issue of Tim's sloppy passes. Tim had learned what the other members of the team had learned before: that Nick did not intend to let his fame interfere with the present football setup. He was playing football, as the other Cougars were, for the fun of it. He had obviously put the idea across and had made it stick.

The immediate effect of Tim's discovery was apparent. Hogan continued to drill the Cougars in pass patterns, but Tim's passes now began to find the target. No longer faced with the exacting problem of throwing the ball to a status symbol, Tim's muscles limbered up, his nerves settled down, and his timing smoothed out nicely.

When Hogan sent Tim and Nick to the side line for a short rest, Nick complained good-naturedly, "You're making it too easy for me."

"I was scared of you at first," admitted Tim.

"Aw, nuts!" said Nick. Then, thoughtfully, he added, "I can see how you might be. Reputations are funny things, especially in their effect on other people. Frankly, I was scared myself when I started playing with these guys. I was afraid they wouldn't accept me as just another football player. I'm flattered that they have. The men on sandlot teams actually seem closer to each other than those on college teams. You've probably noticed that already."

"I'm afraid I haven't," Tim said dryly.

Nick flushed. "There goes my big foot in my big

mouth again. I didn't stop to think you haven't played college ball."

"It's okay. It's taking me a little time to get used to the idea that I went off half-cocked and made a fool of myself."

"You talk as if it's too late to do anything about it."

Tim scarcely knew Nick, yet there was something so fundamentally likable about him that Tim felt the barrier he had built around himself weaken. It was nice, after all, to find someone his own age who seemed sincerely interested in his problem. But it was not the proper moment to take advantage of his find.

"It's not too late," said Tim ruefully, "but first I've got to decide what to do. In the meanwhile, I'll play football."

"Good idea. Football is good medicine. That is, for most people," he qualified, "but I'm not so sure it's good for me."

"How come?"

Nick shrugged. "My father talked me out of pro football, which means I should be spending all my time at the plant learning the business. The trouble is, I can't get football out of my system. Dad's been pretty good-natured about it, but there's no telling how long his patience will last. I'm pushing my luck by playing with the Cougars, and I hope it holds out. We're going to have a real team this year with you at quarterback."

"I hope you're right."

"I know I'm right. You throw a mighty good pass, and it'll get better. I ought to know. You throw a light ball, fast enough to reach the receiver in time, but easy to handle when it gets there. Those bullet passes that some quarterbacks throw may reach the target a fraction of a second sooner, but they're murder to handle, and even the best receivers will miss one now and then. If you can run the team the way you can pass the ball, the Cougars will be hard to beat."

"It's a big if," said Tim. "But it won't be long before we'll know."

It wasn't very long. When Bart Hogan started serious scrimmage in preparation for the Cougars' opening game, he permitted Tim to take complete charge at quarterback for extended periods. Hogan offered neither criticism nor approval. He watched intently, using his own experience to weigh Tim's talent as a team leader. Tim could only guess at what was going on in Hogan's mind, but for the most part Tim was certain that his football instincts were still sound and were growing sharper each day. When Hogan finally expressed his opinion on the matter he confirmed Tim's optimism.

"You've still got it, Tim. Call it a natural gift, instinct, or football sense, it all boils down to the same thing—a good quarterback. Some have it and some don't. You happen to be one of the lucky ones."

"Well—thanks," acknowledged Tim. "I don't know what it is either, but I sure like the way it feels."

"That's a good word for it, feeling. A fine quarterback has a feeling for the team as a whole and for each man on it. He senses when the team is up and when it's down. He can sense when individuals are having better-than-normal days and when they're not, and he fits the pattern of his plays to what he can expect from the men."

"Don't give me any big ideas about myself," warned Tim.

"If they get too big I'll bat them down," said Hogan with a grin. "And, come to think of it, this might be a good time to start."

Tim waited without too much apprehension. After a moment, Hogan went on, "It's just as important for a quarterback to have a feeling for the opposing team as it is for him to know his own men. He has to sense what's going on across the line, so he can hit the weak spots and steer clear of the strong ones."

Tim nodded agreement.

"Up to now," continued Hogan, "you've been calling signals against a familiar team. You know the men, their habits, and their individual abilities. By this time you should come close to knowing how they think. In other words, your job has been relatively easy compared to what it'll be when you face a strange team. Does that make sense?"

"It sure does."

"There's a fast turnover in sandlot teams. They're not like college or even high school teams, where the best players are usually on the same team for several years. We have a few volunteer scouts who can help us some. I can probably help a little, too, by tipping you off to the coaching systems of the coaches I know—that is, if they're still coaching the same teams this year. But we're going to find plenty of new problems in every game we play. And they won't be easy games. Keep that in mind. We're in a tough eight-team league. They play hard football and they play for keeps. You'll find it out next Saturday when we open against the Danville Rocks."

Chapter Four

On the following Saturday, Tim learned that Hogan's remarks were well-founded. The visiting Rocks were tough, very tough. They were short on polish and coordination, but made up for a lack of finesse with the reckless fury of their play. Being more than willing to risk life and limb, the Rocks received the kickoff, then uncorked a savage ground attack that carried them across the goal line. They missed the try for the extra point, but seemed content with their six-point lead. Their attitude implied that they could add to it at will.

The fans were standing behind ropes along the side lines. Danville had sent a crowd of several hundred whose noise suggested twice that number when their boys handed them a touchdown. The Cougar fans were far less happy. They made a few hopeful noises of their own, however, when the Cougars deployed to receive the kickoff.

The message the hometown fans were sending out was very clear indeed. They wanted a touchdown, and they wanted it fast. They were looking for some prompt proof that the Cougars did not intend to get pushed around all afternoon. Hope rested largely on Tim Barlow, who, as quarterback and leader of the team, was supposed to improve the bad situation right away.

The responsibility so suddenly thrust on Tim sent him into a state of shock close to panic. Once more the knowledge hit him hard that he was not playing against high school kids. It was one thing to face the fact in scrimmage, another thing entirely, as Hogan had pointed out, to face it in a game played for keeps. He moved to the deep spot near the goalposts, hoping fervently the kickoff would not come to him.

It came directly to him. He let his breath out in a startled snort, grabbed for the ball, and almost bobbled it. Controlling it after a short juggling act, he started upfield at a speed that showed small regard for his blocking. He cut for the side line at the wrong time, and a herd of Rocks clobbered him from the middle and both sides. After they brought him down, he could hear them chuckling happily.

One big gorilla, with a two-day growth of whiskers, asked him, "Is this the way you used to run the ball in high school? Keep it up—we like it."

It was a tip-off that the Rocks knew Tim by reputation and planned to needle him as part of their strategy. It was not good strategy, because it made Tim mad. The mauling he had received from the Rock tacklers was also beneficial, reminding him he was in a football game, not a scrimmage session. He began to think in football terms, remembering Hogan's statement that a quarterback must waste no time learning all he can about the opposition.

The first thing that came to his attention was a simple, elemental fact. Flushed with the success of their speedy touchdown, the Rocks were wound up tight, poised with hair-trigger eagerness. They were taut and ready when they moved to their defensive spots. Tim flushed the Cougars quickly from the huddle with the deliberate intention of wasting most of the twenty-five seconds on the line of scrimmage before taking the snap from center.

It was a good move—a little sneaky, but sound. The wait was too long for the Rock left guard. He twitched a few times then plunged across the line. The head linesman blew his whistle for an offside penalty, and the Cougars were presented with a five-yard gain without loss of a down. Back in the huddle Tim called the same play he had called before—a draw play.

It was a natural, as Tim had hoped it would be. This time he took a fast snap from center, and the Rocks, wary of another offside penalty, remained frozen for an instant.

When they found they had been tricked, they exploded into angry action. The left guard, hoping to atone for his earlier blunder, charged obediently and unopposed into the Cougar backfield where Mel Harper, the right half, cut him down with a hard block.

Tim faked a hand-off to his left half, Max Cotton, who hit the left side of the line and pulled the Rock linebackers in that direction. Flipping the ball to his big fullback, Joe Tabor, Tim then spun about to lead Tabor through the hole that had been left by the Rocks' eager-beaver left guard. He blocked out a surprised linebacker, and Tabor carved out a twelve-yard gain.

While the Rocks were still talking to themselves, Tim upset their balance even more. He sent Max Cotton on a fake off-tackle plunge, then kept the ball himself. His own fake around left end drew most of the defenders in that direction. Just short of the scrimmage line, he plowed to a stop, then angled a pass across to Nick, who hauled it in and peeled off another eighteen yards before the Rock safety man ran him out of bounds.

The drive looked as if it might easily go all the way for a touchdown before the Rocks pulled themselves together. Unfortunately, it did not. Mel Harper sliced through the line on a well-timed cutback, but a Rock linebacker jarred the ball loose with a savage tackle. The Rocks recovered the fumble on their own eighteen-yard line. Harper came to his feet with the stricken look of a man who has nothing more to live for.

Tim reached him first. "Forget it," he said easily. "Everybody drops one now and then. We've got a lot of time yet, Mel. These guys are tough, but we'll lick 'em."

Mel Harper looked relieved. There was a lot of conviction in Tim's tone, so much that Tim himself was surprised. He had intended to console his halfback, but when the words came out he realized that they stemmed from honest belief. He had seen the Rocks in action, not long it is true, but long enough to be assured that they were strong on muscle, weak in experience.

As the game went on, Tim's assurance proved to be well-founded. The Rocks started another drive, no less determined than the first, but not as effective. They ground out two first downs against a stiffening Cougar defense. Replacements brought advice from Bart Hogan on the bench, advice that stalled the Rock advance and forced a kick.

Tim got the Cougars under way again. He was in no great rush to prove that the Rocks could be licked; there was still a lot to learn about the other team. Tim learned it steadily, not by careful tabulation, but by a strange process of assimilation. The knowledge seeped into his mind like water dripping on a sponge, and he absorbed it through no conscious effort of his own. And once he had digested it, the information came back as a sure instinct for the right play at the right time.

In an impressive performance at quarterback, Tim kept the Rocks off balance. He feinted, jabbed, and slugged at them until the confusion he dealt out to the Rock defense was carried to their offense. He was willing to accept some credit for the job, but not too much. There was a lot to work with in the Cougar squad, and he realized that the Rocks were not its match in coaching or in talent. The final score was 33–12.

The immediate effect of the Cougars' victory was pleasant for Tim Barlow until he realized what was going on. The Cougar fans had seen their new quarterback in action and were pleased with what they had seen. They chose to believe the Cougars had defeated a strong team and that Tim's great generalship was the biggest factor in the victory. Tim automatically became a public figure of considerable importance. Fans stopped him on the street to shake his hand. Tim liked it. He permitted himself to enjoy his new position for a while, then forced himself to look the facts straight in the face.

"I'm a hero here in Greytown," Tim announced, using Bart Hogan as a sounding board.

"Something of the sort," agreed Hogan cautiously.

"I'm a hotshot, a big wheel, because they think I can play football."

"I think you can play football, too. You called a mighty fine game against the Rocks. You can't blame the fans for liking what they saw."

"I don't blame *them*," said Tim, "I blame myself. I've been lapping it up like a cat with a dish of cream. If I keep it up I'll be right back where I started."

Hogan nodded. "You're getting through to me."

"So soon it'll be the way it was before. Nothing will matter except football. I think I've got a one-track mind, and a pretty weak one at that."

"Now look, Tim," said Hogan, with a touch of exasperation, "if you want to have a low opinion of yourself, it's your business, not mine. I'll admit you've got a problem, but it's a problem you've got to work out for yourself. Any advice I might give you would be prejudiced, because I want to keep you on this football team. You're mighty valuable to me."

"Thanks," Tim acknowledged dryly. "You're right, of course. I'll probably be better off in the long run if I *do* work it out for myself, and I think the first step is to get a job."

"Good idea. And that's a department in which I *can* help you. I've got some good connections in this town."

"No," said Tim with stubborn pride. "I'm grateful and all that, but I've got to start from scratch."

"That's the right direction," agreed Hogan.

Job hunting was a new experience for Tim Barlow, and not one that he looked forward to. He began to wish he had not been so hasty in rejecting Hogan's offer. At first he was sure a job would be easy to find, because of his new-found importance in Greytown, but the more he considered the celebrity angle, the less it appealed to him. He would be taking the easy way out again if he cashed in on his football reputation. He decided, therefore, to have a try at the largest and most impersonal industry Greytown had to offer, the Greytown Tool Company.

He felt awkward and out of place when he entered the imposing lobby. With stiff legs he moved toward the information desk, behind which sat a young, attractive woman. A nameplate on the desk identified her as Miss Bell.

"May I help you?" she asked pleasantly.

"I'm looking for a job," Tim blurted, unhappily aware that the approach was crude.

Miss Bell, however, appeared interested and helpful. "I'll have to refer you to the personnel department," she told Tim. "I'll see if Mr. Trent is free." She picked up the desk phone and called an extension number. "Mr. Trent? There's a young man here to see you. Yes sir, right away."

She replaced the phone and smiled at Tim. "He's not busy. You'll find him down the right-hand corridor, third office on the left. Go right in."

"Thank you," acknowledged Tim.

He started for Mr. Trent's office, grateful that he still felt like a human being of some stature. His first brush with big business had been fairly painless, and promised to remain so when he entered Mr. Trent's office. There he found a middle-aged man with graying hair and pleasant eyes.

The man rose from his desk, shook hands, and introduced himself. "I'm John Trent."

"Tim Barlow."

Tim was glad that Mr. Trent did not appear to recognize the name. He motioned Tim to a chair across the desk and resumed his own chair in a relaxed manner. There were a couple of shallow stacks of paper on the desk. Mr. Trent took a paper, obviously an application form, from the top of one pile. He placed it in front of him and picked up a pen.

"I must warn you first," said Mr. Trent, "that we have no immediate openings. But our turnover is quite rapid these days, and we're always looking for good people. All right?"

"Yes, sir."

Mr. Trent poised his pen above the form, and said, "We'll start with schooling. What is your scholastic background, Mr. Barlow?"

Tim's throat went dry. "Third-year high school." The answer came out as a confession.

The pen froze above the paper. Mr. Trent shot an almost accusing glance across the desk, as if Tim had tricked him. "You fooled me," he confessed, embarrassed. "I had you figured for a college man."

"Sorry," Tim said tightly. "Shall I go?"

"Not at all," said Mr. Trent good-naturedly. "As I told you, we're always on the hunt for good men, and when we find one there are lots of places we can spot him."

Meanwhile, Mr. Trent was attempting some sleight

of hand. Hoping not to attract Tim's attention, he slid a
paper from the second pile and maneuvered it on top of
the form on which he had been about to write. It was
obviously a form for applicants whose education was
inadequate, men who could not hope to qualify for jobs
which might someday lead to the executive offices. Tim
felt sick; an inner hollowness drained the color from his
face. He had an angry urge to leap up and rush from the
room. With an effort, he controlled himself, knowing that
the fault was not John Trent's, that Mr. Trent was a
courteous, kind man, who had probably been chosen for
the post because of these very qualities.

Tim forced a weak smile and answered a long list of
questions, trying, for Mr. Trent's sake, to hide his own
indifference. The Greytown Tool Company would probably find a job for him in time. As Mr. Trent had said, they
needed good men, even some, Tim decided bitterly, with
strong backs, willing hands, and not too much intelligence.

Chapter Five

When Tim Barlow left the personnel office, he moved with the heavy, aimless stride of a man trying to recover from shock. Nothing could have been more graphic, more revealing, than the separate application blanks. His lack of education could seriously affect his life. He had, in a vague way, recognized his status as a dropout, but not until today had he understood it with such ruthless clarity.

Tim had walked some distance, reaching a turn in the corridor, before he realized he was headed in the wrong direction. Another man, rounding the corner, almost bumped into him.

The man said, "Oops!" Then he exclaimed in surprise, "Tim! What are you doing here?"

Tim's morale at that moment was too low to leave any room for embarrassment. He said, "Hi, Nick. I was looking for a job." Then, as an afterthought, he asked, "What're you doing here?"

Nick stared at Tim before confessing in an apologetic tone, "I work here. My dad owns the joint."

"What?" Tim gasped.

"It's not *my* fault," Nick excused himself.

It took Tim several seconds to absorb the news. "I must be pretty stupid," he finally said. "Maybe my brains are only good for football. It never occurred to me that you were connected with this company. In fact, I've been away so long that I'd almost forgotten that the Jeffer family owned it."

"So much for that," said Nick. "How about the job?"

"They filled out an application for me—one of the day-laborer blanks."

Nick made a wry face.

Tim hurried to explain, "I sound like a sorehead who got the brush-off. It wasn't like that at all. Mr. Trent is a swell guy. He couldn't have been nicer to me if I'd waltzed in there with a Ph.D."

"You in a hurry?" Nick asked.

Tim shook his head. "Merely job hunting."

"That'll wait," said Nick. "Let's go to the cafeteria for a cup of coffee."

"I don't want to take you away from your work," Tim protested mildly.

Nick snorted. "Are you kidding? The work I do

around this place could be handled by anybody. Let's go."

Nick led the way to the company cafeteria, which was deserted at that hour of the morning. When they took their coffee to a table, Nick explained with irony, "No one but important executives like me dare to show their face in here before noon."

While Nick stared at his coffee, waiting for it to cool, Tim realized with astonishment that Nick was not happy, that he had something on his mind and had grabbed this opportunity to talk about it.

"I'm a lousy failure," Nick announced.

The statement struck Tim as amusing, but he overcame the urge to smile. "That makes two of us," he said.

"It's my turn first," said Nick. Then with a sour grin he went on, "Does the poor little rich boy sound sorry for himself?"

"Sort of," Tim conceded.

"You didn't *have* to agree with me," Nick growled. He took a sip of coffee. "Anyway, you're sore at yourself because you dropped out of high school, and I'm sore at myself because I had everything dumped in my lap and won't take advantage of it. Quite a difference, huh?"

"A big, wide gap."

"I've tried, Tim, I swear I have, but I can't get football out of my system. If I could leave it alone, I know I could take a real interest in the tool business. As it is, I'm a bust and everybody in the plant knows it. I've got a big, swank office that I hate. I'm the boss's pampered son, and that's my distinguished position in the company."

Tim stared at Nick for a long moment before saying, "It's funny, Nick, but I feel better now. I don't know why, but I feel better just the same."

"Me too," said Nick. "We're just a pair of poor little lambs who have lost their way. What next?"

"I'll finish high school," Tim announced, as if the idea were entirely new to him. "I'll get a diploma through a correspondence course."

"Good start," Nick approved.

"Start?" Tim repeated, momentarily puzzled. Then, "Oh, I get the point."

"It's one you need to remember," said Nick. "When you go job hunting, there's another big gap between high school graduates and college graduates."

"But why waste time in college if you don't know what you're after?"

"Because a sheepskin has a strong appeal to most employers. They automatically assume a college graduate is smart. A degree opens the door to better jobs and better pay."

"I'll tackle that one when I get to it—if I ever do," said Tim. "And now that my future has been settled, how about yours?"

Nick shrugged. "I'll stick it out a little longer as the boss's son. Meanwhile, I'm going to enjoy this football season, which will probably be my last. I suggest you do the same."

"Why not? What've we got to lose?"

"Nothing," said Nick grimly, "but our self-respect, and neither of us seems to have much of that left anyway."

Tim promptly set about to bolster his remaining self-respect. A long talk with the high school principal was encouraging. He was happy to arrange for a correspondence course through an accredited school, and he outlined a course of study that would give Tim a running start while the details of the correspondence course were being settled.

Tim's next move was to find a job, to swallow his false pride, and to accept any reputable work available. He decided to turn down what chance he might have to join the tool company. Since Nick was one of the officers, as well as a fellow Cougar, he might think that Tim would expect small favors from him. Tim wanted to avoid an association of that sort. Instead, he went to work in a filling station.

Tim was reasonably content for a while. For the first time in his civilian life he was self-supporting, which was in itself a step in the right direction. He attacked his studies with a reluctance held over from his high school days, and after a few false starts and a few rough sessions, he came up with a bit of knowledge so profound that he needed several days to analyze and understand it.

The books he studied were not fierce dragons with long teeth. Some subjects, true, were not very palatable. On the other hand, they did not scare the daylights out of him as they had in the past. His previous go-around with textbooks had been compulsory, as if he had been dragged to them with a chain around his neck. Correspondence study was different; voluntary and self-imposed conditions made the books seem much less formidable than they ever had before.

When Tim accepted this revelation, he realized he had crossed a barrier of considerable height. The books appeared more willing to give up their secrets. He began to learn the art of studying. He found that concentration paid big dividends and transformed a jumbled mass of letters into words that made a lot of sense. Once the message of the words seeped in, he began to believe that he was not as stupid as he had feared.

His greatest and most satisfying outlet, though, was football, and Tim had every reason to be satisfied with the way he was playing. Physical maturity helped him. He was strong and durable, hard as rocks. Blended with these assets was his football instinct, a natural gift that flourished under the tutelage of Bart Hogan.

Tim was not the only one to benefit from Hogan's coaching. The result was a fine football team that excited the hope and imagination of the players and of the fans. It was, beyond a doubt, the greatest of all Cougar teams.

The Cougar attack was spearheaded by Tim Barlow and Nick Jeffer, a rare passing combination. The two men possessed an almost uncanny ability to anticipate each other's moves. They were a constant threat and served to keep an opponent's defense off-balance. When the opposition double-teamed, or even triple-teamed Nick, however, Tim could pass with confidence to Ray Coburn, the man Tim had replaced at quarterback.

Alone, Tim was a major threat on every play. His ball handling became smooth, accurate, and tricky. The Cougars' limited number of plays included keeper plays, which called for Tim to carry the ball after he had faked a pass to draw the defenders out of position. There were also option plays, which permitted Tim to carry the ball on occasions when the pass defense became too tight. When Tim took off along the ground he was always dangerous, because he had deceptive speed and a limber, shifty style of running.

Although the Cougars had never been able to boast an undefeated season, it began to look as if they might bring one off, a happy possibility that built increasing tension in the fans. Excited as they were, however, they had to accept it as no more than a possibility; even when the Cougars kept their record clean down to the final game, their success was just a curtain raiser to the big one—the game against the Harper City Rams.

Greytown and Harper City were neighbors, some

twenty miles apart, and natural rivals. Booming with industry, Harper City was about three times the size of
Greytown, and it had a larger city's tendency to adopt a
patronizing attitude toward its smaller neighbor. The con-
descension galled the citizens of Greytown, even though
they seldom had a chance to do anything about it. Under-
standably, their optimism soared at the chance that their
beloved Cougars might shellac the Rams.

Beating Harper City would not be easy. The Rams
had dominated the conference for the past five years,
recruiting their teams with an arrogance that ignored the
indignation of clubs whose resources were far less than
those of Harper City, and whose ethics were probably
higher. It was not unusual for college football stars to
announce plans to live in Harper City and to find impressive jobs without effort. It was hardly a coincidence that
these same stars played football for the Rams. It was
rumored that the men were really paid for playing football,
not for doing their nominal jobs. No one could prove it.
The Rams, according to their bland assertion, were all
above reproach.

In the final days of preparation for the game against
the Rams, the growing excitement of the Cougar fans
swirled about Tim like a whirlpool. That he was the Cougars' big ace in the hole was a belief he could accept by this
time without letting it upset his balance.

As the game approached, he experienced periods of

disturbing, sober thought, which left him frightened and unsure of anything. He was not worried about the part expected of him in the game itself. He anticipated it with grim pleasure. What worried him was the conclusion of the game, no matter who won. When the game was over, something would be ended for Tim Barlow, a brief part of his life in which football had partially helped him to forget, or at least to sidetrack, major issues. He would have to face them then. He would be compelled to fill the gaping void football would leave in his existence as best he could. The prospect was not pleasant.

But Tim's concern for what lay ahead was shocked into numbness by Bart Hogan before the Cougars' final light scrimmage got under way.

Seeming ill at ease, almost uncertain of himself, the coach called him aside. He said, "I've stuck my neck out, Tim, maybe a lot farther than I had a right to. You'll have to decide."

"I'll do my best," said Tim, thoroughly puzzled.

"I've meddled in your future," confessed Hogan. "I've invited a pro scout to watch the game on Saturday."

Tim stared for a moment before stammering, "You—you *what?*"

"You heard me," Hogan said defensively. Then he hurried on, "I still have some good connections with my old club, the Mohawks. I think you're pro material, and they took my word for it. I didn't know until this morning that the scout would be in Harper City. He's a friend of mine, Matt Seely."

Tim's thoughts tumbled crazily around. "But why would a pro scout be interested in a sandlot team?" he asked.

"For one thing," said Hogan with more confidence, "no manager of a pro team will ever forget that Johnny Unitas, one of the great quarterbacks, was a product of the sandlots. And for another thing, the Mohawks still think I'm a good judge of football talent."

They were standing in the end zone. Tim moved a few steps toward the goalposts. He placed a hand on one of the uprights, hoping the feel of something solid might help his mind return to normal.

He finally turned to Hogan, saying, "You sure tossed a bomb at me. It'll probably sound stupid of me to admit that I've never given pro football a thought, but it's the truth. It's a new idea, and I don't know whether it's good or not."

"That's understandable, and I expected you to feel that way. I want you to know I've given the matter a lot of thought, so you won't get the idea I went off half-cocked. I've lined up a few ideas that seem sensible to me and might help clear things up a bit for you. Want to hear them?"

"Of course I do."

"To start with, I don't think I'm too far wrong in

assuming that you're still uncertain about a lot of things."

"That's a mild way of putting it," said Tim.

"You'll get a high school diploma—a good start. After you get it, I assume that you'll start thinking of college."

"Could be," said Tim without too much conviction.

"Your father could probably afford to send you to college."

"I wouldn't let him," Tim said promptly, "not after what I've already done to him."

"Okay, I had that figured too. You have three more choices. You can work your way through or go in on a football scholarship, and you've already told me why you don't want a scholarship. I can see your point and I agree with you."

"And the third choice?"

"Pro football. If you make the grade."

"Keep shooting."

"Pro football may give you a more active interest in a college education, and, if so, it will give you more time to decide on a course of study. It will provide plenty of money for your tuition, together with plenty of time off-season for you to go to school. If you don't go to college, there's always the chance that you can stay in the big time long enough to save money for a sound financial backlog when you get out. How does all this sound to you?"

Tim let his breath out slowly. "It makes me dizzy," he confessed. "It also sounds exciting and too good to be true."

"It may not be true," warned Hogan bluntly. "Pro football is big business and it doesn't throw money away on many long shots. I told you Matt Seely was a good friend of mine. That doesn't mean it will affect his judgment when he scouts a player. He can't afford to make mistakes, because his own job is at stake. He's a seasoned scout of long experience. I'm not. He may not agree with me that you're big-league material."

"I hope he does," said Tim shakily. "I sure hope he agrees with you."

Chapter Six

Tim tried hard to accept Bart Hogan's warning. He recognized the danger of letting his expectations get out of hand, of permitting them to soar so high that the crash, if it did come, would be devastating. It was impossible, of course, to restrain his hopes entirely or to curb the flight of his imagination. Pro football! Magic words with power to cause the rebirth of his ambition.

When the first surge of excitement calmed a bit, Tim was able to regard the opportunity ahead of him more soberly. By applying ruthless logic, he forced himself to admit that his interest in pro football was not motivated by all the factors Hogan had discussed. The football part was fine, great. If he made the grade, he could keep on playing football, which was still the biggest interest in his life. The other considerations, self-advancement, educational opportunities, and all that, were no more than dim outlines to be filled in when the time came—if it ever did.

There was no way for Tim to know whether or not Hogan wanted the scout's visit to remain a secret. To be on the safe side, Tim accepted the news as confidential, even though it was hard to keep it bottled up inside himself. It came as a relief when the local paper put the information into print the next morning, bragging that one of the Cougars' players was good enough to attract a big-league scout to Harper City for the game.

There was no scrimmage for the Cougars on the day before the game. Their schedule called for only a few limbering-up exercises and some skull practice on the blackboard in the dressing room. As Tim walked toward the field, Nick's low-slung sports car pulled up beside him.

"Want a ride?"

"Sure."

Once in the car, Tim asked, "You've heard about the scout, haven't you? It was in the paper this morning."

"What scout? I didn't read the paper."

"A scout from the Mohawks will be in Harper City tomorrow to watch the game. Hogan talked him into coming."

The car swerved slightly. "Are you kidding?" Nick demanded.

"No, it's the straight stuff. Hogan told me."

"A scout! A big-league scout," said Nick, his voice

unsteady with excitement. "It just might be that . . ." his voice trailed off. He hauled in a deep breath. "How crazy can I get?" he said bitterly. "I'm smart enough to know that Hogan asked him down here to take a look at you, but for a moment. . . . Well, I forgot I was a big businessman."

"Tough, real tough," said Tim with irony.

Nick grinned. "Tougher than you think, mister. Just the same, Tim, I'm really glad for you, and I mean it. It might solve *your* problem at any rate. I envy you. I know you've got the stuff to make the grade."

"Thanks. I hope you're right. We'll find out tomorrow."

Tim did not sleep well that night, which did not surprise him. On the following day he would come up against his moment of truth, the most important he had ever faced. The magnitude of the event was frightening. It had so many ramifications that he could not possibly run all of them to earth. He finally sank into a restless sleep and felt pretty well dragged out when morning came.

Willing volunteers drove the Cougar squad to Harper City. The game would be played in the Municipal Stadium, an elaborate plant for a town the size of Harper City. Concrete bleachers on either side of the field could accommodate the many fans expected for the game, including the host of wild-eyed rooters who would make the short trip from Greytown.

The dressing room was better than the one to which

the Cougars were accustomed, but they were scarcely aware of such details at the moment. Even though Tim had reasons of his own to be wound up tight, he sensed that the Cougars were vibrating at a higher pitch than he had noticed before previous games, proof enough that the Ram-Cougar battle was the big one, the final showdown.

Gradually Tim became aware of another fact that added further to his mounting pile of worries. The Cougars kept looking involuntarily in his direction, and their glances carried the same message: Tim Barlow was their big ace in the hole, their secret weapon, the man who would lick the Rams for them.

Tim was willing to acknowledge his value to the team in a modest sort of way. What alarmed him was that the Cougars might get the idea of his invincibility so firmly rooted in their mind that they would depend on him *too* much, that their faith might be so great as to obscure the need for their help. If that situation developed, and Tim failed to carry the huge load, the Cougars could conceivably blame him for the loss. Tim finally managed to put that particular worry out of his mind. When the game got under way would be time enough to consider it.

The Cougars got a thunderous welcome from their fans when they went out for their warm-up. The Rams were already on the field, and Tim's heart took an extra hop when he saw the size of their players and the confidence with which they worked. The Ram fans were openly patronizing in their attitude toward the visitors, accepting the evidence of the past few years that the Rams were unbeatable in their league.

Tim was soon aware that the Rams had heard a lot about him and accepted him as the only threat to their undefeated season. Some of them regarded him but briefly, while others made a point of standing still to stare at him, a hammy bit of acting obviously intended to chill the marrow of Tim's bones. It was sound, though clumsy, strategy, because a timid quarterback is an invitation to defeat. Tim easily ignored the stares, however. In the first place, they did not alarm him. In the second place, he kept wondering where the scout, Matt Seely, was sitting. High up in the bleachers, probably, where he could watch the play more easily.

Tim was not happy about the way his nerves were jumping when kickoff time drew near. As the captains went to the middle of the field for the toss, Tim found it hard to breathe. The coin glittered in the air. The Rams won the toss, and when they elected to receive, Tim's breath came out in a grateful rush. He would be able to get a little defensive action, enough to settle his nerves, before being called on to lead the Cougars. He would also be able to watch the Rams in play and to make mental notes on their offensive.

Nick Jeffer kicked off for the Cougars. He booted a good one off the tee, and a Ram halfback gathered it in on his five-yard line. The Cougars took off downfield as if a pack of hunting dogs were on their heels, and the clash of meeting bodies could be heard above the screaming of the fans.

The Rams' blocking on the runback seemed a little careless. Either that or their confidence was riding much too high. Clearly they had underestimated the Cougars' savage charge. Their blocking was cut down before it had a chance to be effective, and Ray Coburn, the left end, sliced in to drop the runner on the sixteen-yard line. The Ram fans didn't like it, but the Cougar fans liked it very much indeed.

Though annoyed, the Rams themselves did not seem particularly concerned over the short runback. Their attitude suggested that they believed the Cougars had been lucky, that they were willing to go along with the old theory that even a blind pig can find an acorn now and then. They came out of the huddle with precision. A fast snap almost took the Cougars by surprise as the quarterback, Clem Hack, probed the Cougar line with the fullback plunge inside tackle. The Cougars absorbed most of the punch, but a linebacker had to bring the runner down for a four-yard gain. An end sweep went for seven yards and a first down. The Ram fans felt better.

The Rams' opening attack was impressive, but, Tim reasoned, not necessarily disastrous. It provided the Cougars with some useful information, specifically that the

Rams had a hard-hitting line and a fast backfield. They had heard all this from Bart Hogan, but nothing sinks in as effectively as a firsthand lesson. The Cougars were learning the hard way.

Hogan had warned his men about Clem Hack in particular. Hack had built quite a reputation for himself as a quarterback in a small Midwestern college. He had been good enough to rate a tryout with a big-league pro team, but had not been quite good enough to win a contract. Hack was nevertheless a formidable threat in a sandlot league. From the little Tim had seen so far, Hack handled the ball well and appeared to control the Rams with a firm hand.

The Rams had another strong asset in their right end, Stan Kruger, another former college star. They also had three big ex-college men in the line and another in the backfield. They were loaded with talent, and they promptly tried to make the most of it. Tim had to rely entirely on his hunches calling defensive signals, until he formed a more workable impression of the Rams' offensive pattern.

It now occurred to him that Hack might call a draw play. It seemed reasonable that the Ram quarterback, having carved out two impressive gains, might figure the Cougars to be overeager to plug up the holes in order to stop a third gain. He did not overlook the chance of a pass even this deep in their own territory. Hack had a good arm, and Kruger was a good receiver. Tim faced the Cougars while the Rams were in their huddle.

"Watch for a draw," he told them. "Could also be a pass, so Nick and I will hold back and look for one."

The Rams came to the line and went into their crouch. This time the count was long to tempt some jittery Cougar to jump offside. Hack took the snap from center, then faded back as if looking for a receiver. Tim sensed the fake, because Hack had not faded far enough to make his act convincing.

Furthermore, a charging lineman came barging into the Cougar backfield. He left a wide, tempting gap in the Ram line intended to lure the Cougar right guard, Dave Grant, into the Ram backfield, where he could be rendered useless. Grant, however, failed to take the bait. When Hack tucked the ball into his fullback's belly and the fullback slammed hard toward the hole that was supposed to be there, Dave Grant was there instead, braced and ready. He blasted the Ram fullback with a tackle hard enough to jar the ball loose. It bobbled for a moment on the ground, but Clem Hack was first to reach it. The play went for a four-yard loss, which was better for the Rams than a lost ball.

By this time, the Rams were beginning to get the idea that they were not on the football field to enjoy a picnic. They regarded the Cougars with more respect, settled down to some old-fashioned, hard-nosed football, and regained the four lost yards with a power play up the middle. On third down, ten to go, a pass seemed more than logical, and the Cougars loosened their defense a bit to guard against it.

They were caught flat-footed. Hack took the snap from center, faked a hand-off to his halfback, then rolled out to the left. His two ends and the other halfback were already racing downfield. Tim had moved across to cover the Ram left end, trying at the same time to keep an eye on the direction of the pass. One of these backward glances revealed the unpleasant fact that Hack had exercised his privilege on an option play. Hack was carrying the ball himself, and carrying it all too well.

Tim peeled off from his self-assigned job of covering a receiver. He cut back toward the middle where Clem Hack was weaving his way through the Cougar defense with a stylish brand of loose-legged running that was downright alarming. Tim got to him just as Hack had worked his way past everyone else. Beyond Tim there was nothing but pay dirt.

Tim checked a quick urge to rush the man, knowing that Hack was too slippery to be hauled down by an overeager tackler. Moving with short, quick steps, which kept his balance in control, Tim did not watch Hack's tricky legs nor his head nor his eyes, which could all be used in faking. Instead, Tim kept his eyes on Hack's belt buckle, which would give brief warning if Hack actually did change direction. He veered off within a few strides of Tim. Tim shifted his weight to meet the change, then drove in hard. His shoulder slammed into the proper spot. His arms hooked hard around Hack's body, and the two of them went down together.

When the pair untangled and regained their feet, Tim was puzzled by Hack's behavior. He acted as if he had been stopped by a heavy barrier rather than by a human being. He didn't even glance at Tim. His eyes instead moved promptly toward the grandstand and Tim, following the direction of his gaze, noted that it was centered on the press box atop the stadium. With curiosity Tim turned his own eyes in that direction, and suddenly the small mystery was solved.

A man in a dark suit was sitting in the corner of the press box. He was training a pair of binoculars on the field, and in a flash of intuition Tim was certain of the man's identity—Matt Seely, the Mohawk scout. He accounted for Hack's odd behavior. Hack undoubtedly knew of Seely's presence and must have known where he was seated. It was safe to guess that Hack had not abandoned hope of becoming a pro, and that this unexpected opportunity to perform before a scout was heaven-sent. His quick glance at the press box could only mean, "How did you like that bit of action, Mr. Scout? Keep your eyes on me, and you'll see plenty more."

The discovery was disconcerting to Tim Barlow. It

put the spotlight on his own performance. In the first heat of action he had almost forgotten about Seely, but now that Hack had called the scout to his attention, Tim began to feel like a bug under a microscope, a feeling he promptly recognized as not conducive to good football. Another, more constructive, thought hit him then. If Matt Seely's scrutiny could affect his football for the worse, then surely it might affect Hack in the same way. It was something to watch for and to study.

Tim's first concern, however, was to stop the Rams' drive. At this stage it would not be easy. Hack's run had gone for eighteen yards and put the Rams in a position where they could open up their bag of tricks. It had also served a more dangerous purpose by boosting the Rams' morale to the point where, for the moment at least, they were able to believe themselves invincible. Their confidence was an intangible force that Tim, even with his limited experience, could feel quivering in the air about him.

The Cougars did the best they could. They put up a dogged fight, but the Rams kept grinding out the yards. They also got some breaks, as is apt to happen when a team feels it cannot be stopped.

One of these breaks came on a third down, eight to go. The Cougars had held a line plunge to two yards. Nick Jeffer had broken up a side-line pass. Hack tried another pass on third down, a buttonhook up the middle. The receiver ran his pattern well enough, but the Cougar line pressured Hack into getting rid of the ball too soon. He drilled a hard one, which reached the receiver just as he made his turn. He made a frantic grab—too late. The ball hit him on the chest and blooped into the air. By sheer luck it came down in his hands as he stumbled toward the line of scrimmage, and the play became a completed pass for a gain that brought the chains out from the side line. It was a first down by an inch or so, on the Cougar seventeen-yard line.

A pair of power plays on the ground gained six yards. The Cougars were holding well and learning fast. Clem Hack ran again on third down, another slick keeper play, and made a first down on the six-yard line. Once again Tim noted Hack's quick look of self-approval directed toward the press box. The binoculars, as usual, were trained on the play.

Joe Tabor, the captain, called time out to give his men a breathing spell. When the Cougars had gathered in a group, Tabor asked, "How about it, Tim?"

"We've slowed them down a lot," said Tim. "It's time to stop them. I think we can. Just keep your eyes peeled for anything."

It was broad advice, but the best Tim could give them at the moment. The Cougars held a line plunge to two yards. It was a good start. Their first break came on the next play. The Ram left guard jumped the gun. The

Cougars gladly accepted the five-yard penalty, which put the ball back on the nine-yard line. Hack faked a pass and kept the ball again, gaining back four of the five yards lost on the offsides penalty. With the ball on the five-yard stripe, the Cougar line stormed in to hold a cutback plunge to a yard gain.

On fourth down, goal to go, the Rams decided to pass up the chance for a field goal. The Cougar line dug in. The Rams came out of the huddle into an unbalanced line to the right. Hack took the snap from center, then started fast toward the right end with lots of blocking out in front of him. The Cougars, accepting Hack as the Rams' major threat, swung defensively in that direction just as they were supposed to do. The reverse fooled them completely. The Ram wingback passed Hack running in the opposite direction. Hack flipped the ball to him and the wingback, sprinting around the weak side, crossed the goal line standing up.

Tim had been taken in as badly as the other Cougars. He felt like a fool, but there was nothing he could do about it now. His outraged teammates' fierce effort to break up the try for the extra point failed. The Rams went into an early 7–0 lead.

Chapter Seven

Tim chose to believe the Cougars' anger was an excellent omen. A march such as the Rams had just staged might easily have affected his team the other way. It might have introduced an element of doubt, causing the Cougars to wonder if the Rams might be too tough for them to handle. As it was, the Cougars seemed to think they were about to prove the Rams could not get by with such a trick.

The Cougars' righteous wrath wore off fast, however. It was replaced by an alarming smugness, a complacency that scared the daylights out of Tim, because he recognized its cause. When the Cougars deployed to receive the kickoff, it was not hard to interpret the fond glances the other players sent in his direction as he waited near the goal line. Their looks seemed to say, "Wait till those cocky Rams get a load of the surprise we've got in store for *them*. Wait till we turn our boy Tim Barlow loose!" They were acting like a bunch of kids about to open Christmas presents.

Tim's alarm had but a short time to grow before the kickoff. It was a fine boot up the middle. Tim scarcely had to move before the ball came tumbling into his arms.

When he started upfield, waiting for his blockers to get organized, his suspicions were confirmed. The Cougars, after looking back to be sure Tim had the ball, started happily to clear a path for him. They were not loafing; they merely had supreme confidence in the man behind them.

In their complacency, the Cougars overlooked some important facts: that they had not met a team of the Rams' caliber this season, that the Rams had already tasted blood, and that the Rams were playing before their hometown fans. Added up, they made a formidable sum and sent the Rams ferociously to the attack. They hacked big holes in the Cougars' blocking and hauled Tim down on the fourteen-yard line.

The Cougars were surprised. Some of them also looked reproachfully at Tim. Tight-lipped, Tim said nothing. He could not bring himself to blame his teammates, because he knew their intentions were the best. He also knew they had let themselves slip into a dangerous mental groove, and that something had to be done to jolt them out of it. Unhappily, Tim could not come up with an inspired solution.

The only thing he could think of was another move

to convince himself beyond a doubt that the problem actually existed. He called his own signal in the huddle, a fake pass and a keeper, knowing it was not the best play under the circumstances, since the Rams would be justified in expecting a running play rather than a pass. Nevertheless, it was essential for Tim to find out as soon as possible what was going on in the Cougars' minds.

The play broke well enough. The Cougars' line charge was reasonably good. The right guard came out fast to join the blocking on the end sweep, and for a brief time everything looked hopeful. For a very brief time. Mel Harper, the right half, threw a sloppy block at the Ram end who came storming in at Tim, forcing him to cut back toward the scrimmage line. Things still might have been set up for a short gain except for another poor block aimed at a Ram linebacker. Added to the poor blocking was the fact that the Rams had been coached to zero in on the Cougars' main threat, Tim Barlow. The Rams downed him for a two-yard loss. Quick anger helped Tim come to a decision. He called time out, walked back toward the goal line, and motioned the Cougars to follow him.

"I hate to say this," he told them grimly, "because I may be dead wrong. From where I sit, though, it looks as if you guys aren't holding up your end."

Tim saw a quick wave of resentment travel through the Cougars. He had expected it. He checked their denials with an impatient gesture.

"I know the reason for it," he went on, "and I'm flattered. I really am. The trouble is, you think I'm a lot better than I am. I'll admit I've had some good breaks during the season, but right now we're up against the best team we've ever faced. If I'm going to live up to what you expect of me, I'm going to need help and plenty of it."

Tim was grateful to see some of the resentment fading. "There's another angle," he continued. "It's no secret that a big-league scout is here to look me over, and maybe some of you guys think I'm yelling for help so I'll look good to him. Maybe I am. The point is, though, unless we hit hard and fast, we'll lose. I can't do it all myself. In fact, I can't do *any* of it without all the help you men can give me. It's up to you."

Tim was uncomfortably aware that some of the Cougars were not entirely sold. Nick Jeffer sensed it too. "Tim's right," he said. "We're not a one-man team."

Joe Tabor came up with the clincher. "I'll go along with Nick. I dogged it on that last play. I missed a block that would have shaken Tim loose for at least five yards. Some of you others dogged it too." Guilty nods confirmed the accusation. "Okay," the captain told them sharply, "let's play a little football!"

On second down, twelve yards to go, Tim called the same signal in the huddle. The play could either be a good one or a bad one. When he saw some Cougar backs stiffen at his decision, Tim believed his hunch might be right.

Anyway, he had to know about his team, and this was the best way to find out. He also hoped the Rams would not expect the play to be repeated.

If the Rams noticed the new tautness in the Cougars, they spotted it too late. The play broke fast. When Tim started his wide sweep, the Ram end came charging in with too much confidence. Mel Harper, timing his block sweetly, hit him hard and wiped him out of the play. The block gave Tim running room and thinking time. The Ram linebackers, seeing their end out of action, swung over to protect the area. Tim had time to fake a running pass before cutting back swiftly toward the line of scrimmage.

The linemen had a hole for him, and this time, Joe Tabor did not dog it. He whipped through the hole ahead of Tim, and the same man who had avoided Joe before was not so lucky. Tabor cut him down. Tim, running with calculated speed, stiff-armed one man, dodged another, and peeled off eighteen yards before the safety man, Clem Hack, brought him down.

Hack made a fine tackle, good enough, he must have felt, to justify another peek at the press box. Seeing the quick turn of Hack's head, Tim, realized that he, too, had been about to glance proudly up at Seely. Tim was grateful to Hack for the timely warning to keep his mind on football and not on the Mohawk scout. A division of interest at this stage could be disastrous.

On his way back to the huddle Tim tried to analyze the possible effects of his long gain. His conclusions were optimistic. He had to concede, of course, that a certain element of luck is always present in any sizable advance. He had gambled, and the gamble had paid off. The Cougars' faith in Tim was still intact, with the big difference that they understood Tim needed help and that they could give it to him. The run served an added purpose. It informed the Rams that Tim was dangerous on the ground, and as long as they kept the fact in mind, the Cougars' passing game could be more dangerous still.

With the ball on their thirty-yard line, the Cougars could operate more freely, a situation Tim decided to explore at once. He sent Tabor on a fake plunge into the line. He then bootlegged the ball behind his hip and started around the end. The Rams, with the memory of Tim's last run still fresh in their mind, showed little caution in their move to check another run. Tim plowed to a halt. His protection held. He faked a pass toward the left side line, then drilled one to the right side of the field. Nick ran a smooth in-and-out pattern that shook him loose from a defender. Tim's pass reached him near the side line. Nick hauled it in and stepped out of bounds. The twenty-one-yard gain placed the ball a yard inside Ram territory.

The Cougar fans howled with excitement. The Ram fans began to twitter with alarm. The Ram squad was not too happy either. They called time out to talk and to give the red-hot Cougars a chance to cool off a bit. It was good strategy even if it failed.

When time was called in, Tim decided the Ram defense had been loosened up enough to justify a power play. In the huddle he called for an off-tackle slant, but when the huddle broke and Tim got a good look at the Rams coming grimly to the line, he had a strong hunch that a different play might pay off better. The Ram linemen looked as if they had been ordered to do a specific job, and Tim's instinct told him that they were going to put on a blitz. The defensive play made sense. Having accepted Tim as the Cougar badman, the Rams might believe that an effective blitz would clip Tim Barlow's wings.

Tim played his hunch. He changed the signals with a few crisp audibles before taking the snap from center. The instant the ball reached Tim's hands he knew he had guessed right. The Ram line opened holes through which the Ram linebackers charged like buffaloes. Tim encouraged the blitz by fading back with the ball cocked near his ear as if for a long pass. An instant before the blitzers hauled him down Tim flipped a short lateral to Max Cotton, his left half. With most of the Ram defense trying to tear Tim limb from limb, Max had lots of running room. He scooted down the side line for another twenty-one-yard gain.

The Rams had not been gentle in their blitz. When Tim got slowly to his feet he knew he had been worked on and that much of the roughness had been deliberate. He resented it, but not too seriously. He knew that quarterbacks were open targets and that getting mauled by the opposition was an occupational hazard. He was well aware that a quarterback without the ruggedness to absorb such punishment would be of little use to a pro football team. Oddly enough, Tim was glad the blitz had happened. He felt a little shopworn, but the feeling wore off fast. It was good to know that he was built to take it.

He was also glad to know how well his hunch had worked. The rest of the going would not be easy, however. With the ball on their twenty-eight-yard line, the Rams were now in a position to consolidate their defense, to narrow the passing zone, and to deploy their linebackers more effectively. Tim considered all these factors as he concentrated hard on the job ahead. It would be really tough to have the Cougars' drive bog down while it was still running in high gear.

The Cougars had one thing in their favor, just as the Rams had enjoyed the same advantage in their opening drive. Until each team became familiar with the other's tactics, it would have to do considerable guessing. At this stage, the Rams had not had time to spot the strength and weakness in the Cougar offense.

The Rams were alert and on their toes when the Cougars came out of the huddle. The linebackers were well-spaced and poised; the line was taut. The Rams, in fact, were ready for anything, anything except the play Tim called on them. It was the most unlikely play in that field position on first down, ten to go. Tim called a quarterback sneak, a play normally reserved for short, important gains.

Tom Jurgen, his big center, snapped the ball and charged. Tim stayed close behind the formidable bulk, and when Jurgen's drive lost steam, Tim slid away from his human tank and scrambled for a few more yards. The play netted six important yards.

Tim held a fast huddle, sending the Cougars swiftly into an unbalanced line before the Rams had entirely recovered from the trick Tim had played on them. A quick snap from center caught the Ram linebackers moving toward the strong side of the Cougar line. Tim faked a hand-off to Mel Harper, who hit the strong side. Tim completed a half spin, then flipped the ball deftly to Joe Tabor, who was already under way toward the weak side. The timing was accurate and clean. Nick Jeffer and the right guard, Dave Grant, had a hole waiting. Tabor hit it and bulled his way for eight yards before he was pulled down.

The Rams called time out to discuss the dangerous situation. A replacement came sprinting in from the bench, obviously bringing instructions from the coach. The Rams welcomed him with hopeful eyes. They needed help, and they needed it fast. They listened eagerly to the replacement's words.

Tim was thinking hard, even though he realized that one guess was as good as another at that point. With their back to the wall and their defense crowded into such a small area, the Rams could hardly be taken by surprise. There was a chance, of course, that they might be concerned about a running play, because the Cougars had been riddling their line successfully. With no more to go on, Tim made his decision in the huddle.

The Cougars hurried into a tight line with the ends drawn in and the backfield in a standard T, a power formation. Tim faked Max Cotton into the left side of the line, then took a couple of swift, backward steps. Nick was already racing down the side line and Ram defenders were closing in on him to protect against a pass to the coffin corner. Tim, however, did not pass to the corner. Instead, he whipped the ball to a point between the corner and the goalposts. He got the ball away a split second before a big Ram slammed into him. It was a pinpoint pass, a beauty, deliberately high to lessen the chance of its being batted down by the defenders. Nick's catch was equally as great. His timing was exact as he cut in from the side line; he reached the right spot at the right time. He went high into the air, outreaching two desperate defenders. He grabbed the pass and held it for a touchdown. Tim kicked the extra point and tied the score, 7–7.

Chapter Eight

There was jubilation in the Cougar rooting section. Among the Cougars, too, there was elation. It seemed to Tim to strike a jarring note. The men were justified, of course, in being happy, but when they started to show signs of cockiness, Tim believed it was time to be alarmed. He did what he could to warn them before the kickoff.

"Don't kid yourselves," he told the team. "These guys aren't pushovers. They hit us before we had a chance to get a line on their attack. We did the same to them. It won't be so easy next time—not for either of us."

The Cougars nodded dutifully, then lined up for the kickoff. Nick got away a good boot, and the Cougars romped gaily down the field to smother the Ram runback. It did not work out that way. The Rams had learned a few things, too, and they treated the Cougars with respect. No longer overconfident, the Rams hit hard and accurately. The runback reached the thirty-six-yard line before the Cougars stopped it.

Tim had a chance to tell his men, "I told you so. These guys are good. You'd better believe it."

The Cougars required another painful lesson before they were willing to accept Tim's warning, and then it was almost too late. The Rams made a couple of first downs along the ground, bringing the ball to the Cougar thirty-eight-yard line. Then Clem Hack came up with a smart play.

Tim was not entirely sure what tipped him off. It might have been sheer instinct, or it might have been that he probably would have called the same play himself under the circumstances. There was another factor, too, small but significant. When Tim saw Hack's involuntarily glance toward the press box, he was reasonably sure that Hack would be importantly involved in whatever play was coming up, either a run or a pass. His look toward the scout seemed to say, "Now keep an eye on *me*."

When the play broke Tim kept a careful eye on the Ram line rather than on Hack. Once assured that the line was being careful not to get too far downfield, Tim kept his eye peeled for a pass. Hack, swinging wide, might still decide to run with the ball, but the play did not shape up that way. To start with, the defense had swung over to protect against a run. Next an alarming condition developed upfield. The two Ram ends were sprinting toward the end zone. There was no great danger there, because Tim was covering the right end and Nick was covering the left end. The hair-raising part was that a Ram halfback was also sprinting up the middle toward the end zone, and that the middle linebacker, Mel Harper, who was supposed to guard that area against a pass, was still looking for a running play. The Ram halfback was all alone.

Tim was able to visualize the setup from the standpoint of a quarterback. He knew what *he* would do if he had to make a quarterback's decision. The choice was easy. He would fire his touchdown bomb to the unprotected halfback. Tim also knew that he had to put on a good act now, and that he had to be convincing.

The halfback and the end, though keeping pace, were separated by some fifteen yards. Tim watched the halfback from the corner of his eye while pretending to devote his entire attention to the end. The timing had to be extremely delicate. A split second could make all the difference. Tim needed to make his move while the ball was in the air so that Hack would have no chance to change his mind.

As a quarterback it was not too hard for Tim to guess the moment at which Hack would throw his bomb. A quick backward glance confirmed his instinct; the ball was on its way. Not until that instant did Tim make his move. He cut sharply toward the middle of the field, centering his entire attention on the halfback. When the Ram crossed the goal line, checked his speed, and turned to make the catch, Tim had almost reached him. Another backward glance to spot the ball, a long twisting jump, and a reach into the air made contact with the ball. Tim's hand slammed solidly against the leather. The ball sailed out of danger while the Ram stood in openmouthed amazement.

When Tim came back to the line of scrimmage, the Cougars' congratulations had a shaky quality. The boys had had the daylights scared out of them. They had dodged a bullet and had sense enough to blame themselves. Clem Hack, quick to spot the trembling condition of the Cougars, made a poor diagnosis of the symptoms. He sent a play into the line hoping to meet small resistance. Instead, the savage rush of men whose fright had not worn off sent the play for a two-yard loss. On third down Hack tried to run the ball himself. He gained two yards. On fourth down the Rams tried a field goal from a distance too great for their kicker. The ball barely crossed the goal line, and the Cougars took possession once more.

Tim had learned a few things from the Rams' last drive, but when he tried to move the Cougars into high gear again, it became apparent that the Rams had also learned a few things about the Cougar offense. Tim mixed his plays enough to carve out two first downs. Then the Rams stalled the Cougars near the midfield stripe and forced a kick.

There was no more scoring in the period, even

though the ball changed hands several times. One fact was becoming clear, however. The Rams, with their bolstering of college talent, had a definite edge in power both on offense and on defense. It was almost bound to show up in the final score unless some lucky breaks tipped the balance. The catch was that the Rams could have breaks as well as the Cougars.

Tim would not concede that the Rams' edge was in anything but physical strength. He felt that the advantage could be overcome through leadership and close study of whatever weaknesses the Rams might unintentionally reveal. They were gradually showing some flaws, small things that Tim grabbed hungrily and tucked away to be digested.

The weaknesses began to form a pattern. Tim took his cue from Hack's compulsive glances toward the press box, where the big-league scout was watching every play. Tim directed his attention to the other college men. He assumed they would also like to ink their name upon a big-league contract. Watching closely, Tim found what he was looking for.

It wasn't much, not enough to change the complexion of the play so early in the game, but it was there. Some of the Rams were sacrificing close team play in favor of an individual effort that might claim the attention of the scout. They were making their pitch for recognition in small ways that Tim spotted carefully and cataloged for future use. The Cougars seemed to be holding their own fairly well at the moment. Later in the game, however, there might be times when the information Tim was gathering would be desperately needed.

Once convinced that Matt Seely's presence was having its effect upon the Rams, Tim found that his discovery gave rise to an important question. How was Tim Barlow being affected by the scout's presence? Was Tim also showing his awareness in ways that might be noticed by the Rams?

Tim believed that the pressure and excitement of the game had claimed most of his attention so far. He did not deny the possibility, however, that the scout might prove distracting later on. Seely was on hand to watch Tim Barlow. Tim knew it, and he didn't try to deny that. He wanted to impress Matt Seely as much as he had ever wanted anything. What measures could he take, he wondered grimly, to keep his mind on *this* game rather than on possible pro games of the future? The word *pro* gave him the answer.

So far as Tim knew, Seely might not be scouting him as a quarterback. He might be watching Tim with an open mind to decide what all-round talent Tim possessed. If so, it would be a waste of time for Tim to try to emphasize any single feature of his game. He knew, for instance, that top-notch pro quarterbacks are not encouraged to run with the ball except in emergencies, because they are too valuable to risk the chance of injury. A smart quarterback with a fine passing arm can earn his keep without exposing himself to gang tackling.

There was no excuse, however, for Tim to hold back from carrying the ball when strategy called for it. It might be that Seely was on the scout for a ball carrier, a fast breakaway man, who could make maximum use of his blocking and who was hard to down. Therefore, Tim's safest bet was to play the sort of game that would most benefit the Cougars. Having arrived at this decision, Tim found it easier to keep his mind on the game and off the press box.

Unquestionably, the game needed all the concentration he could bring to bear. The Rams, soon aware of their slight edge in power, began to make the most of it. They had a strong bench and a smart coach, who made skillful use of his reserves. Bart Hogan did the best he could with his limited replacements. He gave Tim as much rest as he dared while the Rams were on the attack. Tim made full use of the short rests to brief Hogan on the information he was gathering about the Rams. Hogan listened carefully and nodded his approval.

The second period was a nightmare for the Cougars. Mel Harper bobbled a punt near his own goal line. Before he could recover it, the Rams had downed him on the six-yard line. Max Cotton fumbled on the first play. The Rams recovered. The Cougars put up a savage stand. They held the Rams to four yards in three downs. After a brief conference, the Rams went for the six points instead of trying a field goal.

The Cougars held, stopping the drive with an inch or so to spare. Tim tried to carve out running room, but could only dent the Rams' line for four yards on the first two downs. He kicked on third down, a fine snap punt, which the Rams brought back to the Cougar thirty-four-yard line.

Hogan brought Tim to the bench for another rest while the Rams again started their attack. Tim saw Clem Hack glance at the press box before taking the snap from center. Tim watched the movements of the other Rams and sensed what was about to happen. There was no way for him to warn the Cougars. He could only sit and stare and suffer while Hack whipped a long pass into the hands of an unguarded receiver. The Ram fans exploded happily as the man jogged across the goal line. The Cougar fans had their chance to cheer when the play was called back, and the Rams were slapped with a fifteen-yard penalty for offensive holding.

Tim said hoarsely, "I can't stand it! Please, Coach, send me back in there!"

"Go ahead," said Hogan, mopping cold sweat from his forehead. "I can't stand it either."

The Cougars, even on defense, were more effective when Tim was in the line-up. They forced the Rams to kick. The punt went into the end zone, and the Cougars took the ball on their twenty-yard line, once more too deep in Cougar territory for Tim to take any risk. The Cougars were bone tired and battered, and he could not ask much of them in the final minutes of the half.

Tim had to kick again on third down. The Cougars' weariness at this point proved disastrous. A big Ram tackle sifted through the line and blocked the kick. The Rams recovered on the eight-yard line, and the Cougars dug in for another desperate stand. They were game and willing. They did their best, but it was not enough. The Rams blasted their way into the end zone. They missed the extra point and shrugged it off. They were confident that the game was in the bag and coasted easily through the remaining minutes of the half, which ended with the score 13–7.

Bart Hogan did not permit an air of gloom to settle in the dressing room. His tone was easy, self-assured, as he forced the men to think in terms of victory rather than defeat. He made them relax, and as they shook their muscles loose, Tim watched the miracle that fine conditioning of healthy bodies can produce. The lines of fatigue left the Cougars' faces, and when they went out for the second half, their legs were springy and their shoulders straight.

A rested football team is a fine weapon if handled properly, a fact that Tim recognized and hoped to prove. He reasoned that the Rams, with the picture of a weary Cougar team fresh in their mind, might be taken by surprise if Tim could launch a concentrated attack. Many things, of course, could go wrong with an attack, but Tim refused to let possible errors influence his choice of signals.

The Ram kickoff man did a clumsy job, which, as it turned out, was no great help to the Cougars. The ball came off the tee in a wobbly line drive rather than in a long clean arc. It cleared the first line of defense before it hit the ground and started a series of crazy bounces. Avoiding wild grabs, it skidded to the ten-yard line before Mel Harper could fence it in. He managed to return it to the nineteen-yard line, and there the Rams brought him down.

It was not much of a runback, but Tim promptly decided to turn the fact to his advantage. In the closing minutes of the first half the Cougars had played possession football, because Tim had not dared ask more of a tired team. He had a fresh team now, and he gambled that the Rams would remember his caution when the ball was deep in Cougar territory before.

The Cougars came out of the huddle into a tight, balanced line. Tim took the snap from center, went into a half pivot, and faked a hand-off to Joe Tabor, who slammed outside right tackle. Tim faded a few steps and checked his protection with a quick glance. It was holding beautifully. He stepped into the protection of the pocket and spotted Nick Jeffer running ten yards inside the side line. Nick, according to plan, was permitting himself to be well covered by a backfield Ram. The ball was on its way to a selected target before Nick made his move, a swift cut toward the side line. The ball and Nick reached the target area at the same instant. Nick fielded the pass neatly and managed a few steps down the side line before the Ram drove him out of bounds. The play went for a twenty-two-yard gain.

The Rams, momentarily shaken, were a soft touch for another pass. Tim started around the end for what might have been a keeper. He plowed to a stop instead, then scored a bull's-eye on Nick Jeffer, who had befuddled his defense with a simple buttonhook. It was another advance, this time for fourteen yards and a first down. Tim spared a moment to enjoy the thrill of passing to a great receiver.

Keeping the Cougar drive in motion, Tim bludgeoned the Rams on one play, thrust skillfully at them on the next. He used the Tim-to-Nick combination as a deadly threat to loosen the defense and make it vulnerable to ground plays. He had the Cougars hitting smoothly on all cylinders. No team could run in such high gear for very long, but he tried to prolong the period of sweet coordination as much as possible.

Tim carried the ball himself three times, and the results were satisfactory. His third run brought the ball to the Ram eighteen-yard line, first down. On the opening play he sent Nick into the end zone, and, while the Rams were scrambling frantically to keep Nick covered, the other end, Ray Coburn, was wide open also in the end zone. Tim drilled a chest-high pass into his hands. Ray juggled it an instant, but held on. When Tim kicked the extra point, the Cougars went into the lead, 14–13.

Tim did not expect the Rams to be demoralized by the fireworks he had tossed at them, and he was correct. They were shaken up a bit, of course, but the shock was good for them. It brought them back into the game knowing they no longer dared underestimate the Cougars, and it angered them dangerously.

The Cougars, on the other hand, possessed a one-point lead, which they protected like a cougar mother fighting for her young. They had enough stuff left to weather the third period in style. The teams battled toe to toe with neither one approaching pay dirt. When the Cougars had the ball, Tim tried to ignite the crackling spark that had carried the Cougars to their second touchdown, but he could not.

Chapter Nine

The Rams went to work on Tim in the early stages of the fourth period. A huge, ex-college guard named Borg appeared to have been handed the contract. Obviously experienced in that sort of thing, Borg set about putting Tim out of business. His short, concealed punches after a tackle nearly did the job. Tim's temper almost popped its safety valve. On the next play he was about to retaliate in kind despite the danger of a penalty when he was spared the effort.

Dave Grant, the Cougar right guard, could match Borg pound for pound. A plumber at one time, Grant could bend pipe with his hands. Borg, in his eagerness to cross the line and get to Tim, should have kept a closer eye on Grant. With his hands locked and his elbows at the proper angle, Grant let one elbow come in contact with

Borg's jaw, a legal effort to protect his backfield men. Borg hit the ground, out cold. His teammates finally led him wobbling from the field, and after that no more attempts were made to maim the Cougar quarterback. It was just as well, because Tim had other important things to occupy his mind.

The Rams' superior weight and reserve strength began to make themselves felt early in the final period. They brought a Cougar punt back to their own thirty-five-yard line, then carved out two first downs and placed the ball on the Cougar forty-one-yard line. An offside lineman drew a five-yard penalty against the Cougars. On the first play Clem Hack heaved a long pass toward the left side line.

Tim, covering a potential receiver in the middle of the field, had no chance to reach the spot to which the pass was thrown. But it did not look as if his help were needed; Mel Harper seemed to have the situation under control. He broke up the Ram pass in a way that did not please the field judge, however. His whistle squealed, and he promptly called pass interference against the Cougars. It was one of those hairline decisions that might have gone either way. The official chose to give the Rams possession of the ball on the Cougar twelve-yard line.

The penalty was a heartbreaker for the Cougars, but at least it served to make them mad. They put up a savage stand against two line-crushing plays, which netted the

Rams a scant five yards. On third down Hack tried to be a hero by following his blocking around the left end. The blocking was good, but not good enough. Nick Jeffer refused to be taken out of the play. He slashed into the Ram backfield and dropped Hack for a two-yard loss.

The Cougars were snorting fire. Sensing their determination, the Ram coach decided against taking the long chance of crossing the goal line on the one remaining down and sent his kicking specialist into the game. The Rams went for the field goal and made it good. The Cougars were now trailing 16–14.

As the Cougars went back to receive the kickoff they again appealed to Tim Barlow with their eyes. Their glances said, "Hey, Tim, we're in a lousy jam. You're our last hope."

Tim appreciated their confidence in a grim sort of way. In another way he resented their dependence on him. It made the load he was already carrying a lot heavier, and he hoped that he was equal to the task. He knew it was time to use the information he had gathered, to experiment with the data he had stored away. He had hesitated until now to drag it out for fear that a premature experiment might tip off the Rams to what was going on and give them time to make corrections. The deadline was here, however. He had to use his information now.

He went about it in the first huddle, using the limit of his time to brief the Cougars. He could impart only a few facts at a time, such as the tip that a Ram linebacker was stunting beyond the call of duty, bouncing around like a monkey on a stick in an obvious attempt to call attention to himself. The man was vulnerable and Tim told the Cougars why. A big Ram tackle was also trying too hard to be conspicuous. Tim doled out other small items about the Ram defense in later huddles.

Excitement rose in Tim as he watched the Cougars grasp the meaning of his words and take advantage of them. Nothing spectacular happened, but the Cougars made gradual headway against a team of puzzled Rams. The progress was along the ground, because the Rams had wisely assigned two men to keep an eye on Nick. The Cougars managed three first downs and brought the ball across the midfield stripe before the Rams forced them to kick.

Tim had to be satisfied with that advance. At least he knew that his strategy was workable. The remaining time was discouragingly short, but it might be long enough if the Ram coach, or Hack himself, did not tumble to the system Tim was working on them. If the coach got wise he could make corrections promptly, and the Cougars' advantage would be lost.

With the ball in the Rams' possession, Tim had a chance to brief the Cougars on more of the Rams' bad habits. The Cougars caught on fast. Their defense was made easier by an apparent decision of the Rams to freeze

their two-point lead rather than to take the chance of
losing the ball on an intercepted pass. They hammered out
a pair of skimpy first downs before the Cougars slowed
them to a crawl and forced a kick.

The Cougars started their attack on their own
twenty-three-yard line. Tim assessed the temper of his
men and found it good. They had something working for
them now, a secret weapon that helped relieve their weariness. They believed in Tim and he hoped desperately that
he could justify that faith.

His first job was to assume an air of complete confidence. He accomplished it and watched his attitude rub off
on the men. He brought them sprinting from the huddle
as if they'd never heard of fatigue, aches, and bruises. He
made full use of every weakness the Rams had unwittingly
advertised. He brought the Cougars upfield to a first down
on the Rams' forty-two-yard line.

Just then there was a frantic replacement of Ram
players, a move permissible under the league rules. Tim's
heart sank like a lump of lead, because he understood the
reason for the move. The Ram coach was as smart as Tim
had feared he might be. The coach had finally spotted the
antics that Tim had seen and was taking the offenders out
of the game. They were replaced with men whom Tim had
had small chance to study.

Under normal conditions, replacements of this sort
might not make too much difference against a team that

was on the move and confident that it could keep on moving. In this instance, however, the Cougars credited their present success to Tim's shrewdness in picking flaws in the enemy defense, flaws created by individual performers. What would happen now that these men were no longer in the game?

Tim saw doubt hit the Cougars like a shock wave, and some of it bounced back on him despite his effort to fight it off. He was sure the situation could be remedied in time. Unfortunately, time was not available; it was running out. He dared not count on another chance as good as this one.

Tim aimed the first play at one of the Ram replacements, the right end. It might have worked, but didn't. As soon as the play got under way Tim knew the Cougars were out of gear. The edge of their attack was dulled and lacked close coordination. The screen play gained only a yard. The man who had failed to pull it off looked apologetically at Tim, but apologies did not score touchdowns.

Tim's swift calculation of the odds was not encouraging. He doubted that the Cougars could offer him the tight cooperation needed to maintain the drive. Only one man was left upon whom he could depend completely, Nick Jeffer. The catch was that the Rams were still watching Nick as intently as the weather bureau watches a hurricane.

Tim believed, however, that he had no other choice.

On the second down he tried to spear Nick with a sideline pass. The Rams had him covered like a tent. On the third down Tim tried a short jump pass over the center of the line. Nick came whipping across in time to make connections with the ball. His weaving run handed the Cougars a nice gain, though Tim had the awful feeling that it was not enough for a first down. He sweated the decision out while the chains came in and breathed again when the referee waved his arm toward the Ram goal. It was a first down by an inch or so.

Tim expected orders from the bench at this stage. When none came, he decided to stick with his most dependable asset, Nick Jeffer. An out-and-in pass was hairline close. A defender batted the ball down at the last instant. Tim called another pass play on the second down. The Rams, assuming correctly that the Cougars were making their final desperate effort, put on a blitz that the weary Cougar line could not control. Tim was slapped down for a three-yard loss.

He was weary himself, yet he forced his brain to weigh the Cougars' slender chances. One thing seemed reasonably clear. The Rams would expect a pass, and they would try to stage another successful blitz. With a fresh team he would have tried to capitalize on his hunch by sending someone through the hole the blitzers were sure to leave, but he dared not risk it with the Cougars tired and discouraged. He hoped, however, that the blitz would weaken the Ram defense enough for him to complete a pass. If Nick was covered, there would still be the other end, Coburn, or Harper down the middle.

Tim guessed right about the blitz. It came in all its fury. This time he was ready for it. He angled toward the side line before it reached him, pursuers pounding on his heels as he searched vainly for an open receiver. They were all well covered, leaving Tim with no choice but to run the ball himself.

At least Tim had a temporary advantage. The blitz had depleted the Rams' second line of defense and had left a big hole in the forward line. The other linebackers were defending potential pass receivers. Tim knew that if he could cross the line of scrimmage he was almost certain to get through for a first down.

He cut swiftly toward the hole just as the Ram end made an unsuccessful lunge at him. A remaining lineman, caught off balance, made another lunge. His big hand slapped against Tim's leg pads, jarring Tim off stride, though by no means out of action. Regaining balance, Tim ran with a contained speed that would permit him to change direction with more precision and would also permit a brief study of what lay ahead.

His hopes moved up another notch when he saw the panic of the Ram defenders. They had been caught flat-footed, and they knew it. The men who had been covering pass receivers abandoned the job promptly, but, still shaken by surprise, they were poorly organized for the job of stopping Tim. He side-stepped one of them, stiff-armed another, and was almost in the clear. Not quite. One man remained, Clem Hack, and Hack was dangerous for the reason that he had obviously not panicked. He had kept his head and was waiting carefully for Tim to make the big deciding move.

It looked like the end of the line for Tim. The only move he could think of that had a slim chance of success was a head-on collision. A drive with all his speed behind it might possibly take Hack by surprise and down him long enough for Tim to run right over him. Tim was gathering himself for the big jolt when he heard someone running behind him.

Then a voice said, "I got him, Tim! Hold up!"

Tim checked his speed. Hack saw the trap and moved in fast—too late. A figure angled in past Tim and came in low and hard. Nick timed the block with cold efficiency, wiping Hack from the play, and Tim crossed the goal line standing up.

The furious Rams stormed in to block the try for the extra point, an achievement that turned out to be a waste of time and effort. The Cougars with their 20–16 lead forgot how tired they were, and it is doubtful that a team of full-grown gorillas could have made much headway against them. The Rams had no choice but to go for the long gains through the air in the few remaining minutes. Tim intercepted one of these passes, whereupon the Cougars froze the ball until the game was over.

Chapter Ten

A wildly happy bunch of Cougars filled the dressing room. They gave Tim noisy credit for the win, and Tim's honest protests were drowned out by the hub-bub. He tried to enjoy the same elation that was boosting the men into the clouds, but something held his spirits down, a strong feeling that the victory was not complete—not for him at any rate.

The source of the feeling was not hard to trace. The heat of the game had helped to keep his thoughts in line by preventing him from dwelling too intently on the vast importance of his personal performance in the game. The whole purpose of the game for Tim should have been an effort to impress the Mohawk scout; Tim's whole future might depend on it. He realized now, with a feeling of alarm, that his chief purpose in the game had been to lick the Rams, and that he might possibly have neglected to show himself off to the best advantage.

He tried to reconstruct the game in his mind, but the action came back to him in blurred pictures. He wondered if he dared consult Bart Hogan, then decided against it. There had been no time for Hogan to have a talk with Matt Seely, and at the moment Hogan was fully occupied receiving congratulations from the more important Cougar fans. Maybe Seely would show up in the dressing room. The hope soon died. The Mohawk scout did not appear. Tim's next thought was a heart stopper: maybe Seely had seen plenty and had left for home.

Tim carried his uneasiness to bed with him that night and slept fitfully. By morning he was a scared, unhappy man. When his mother called him to the phone, he held it trembling against his ear.

"Hi, Tim," said the voice at the other end. "Bart Hogan. Sleep well last night?"

"Are you kidding?" said Tim hoarsely.

"I had a long talk with Matt last night. He'd like to see you this morning in my office."

"Did—did he? I mean, what's the—the verdict?"

"Can't say. We talked mostly about old times. Can you be here by nine-thirty?"

"Yes." Tim returned the phone slowly to its cradle. His face was long and his heart was low. He could recognize a gentle brush-off when he heard one. Naturally, Bart

Hogan did not want to give him the bad news. It was Seely's job, and Seely was the man to do it. Tim shaved, dressed carefully, and drank a cup of coffee. It was all he could force down. He arrived at Hogan's office on the dot.

Hogan introduced Tim to Matt Seely, a small middle-aged man with large dark-rimmed glasses and not much hair. He was hardly Tim's idea of a big-league scout, but he was pleasant and amiable enough. Probably just a front, Tim thought morosely, a manner cultivated to break bad news. There was nothing helpful to be learned from Hogan's expression. It was probably the one he wore in court while examining a witness.

Hogan motioned to one of the doors leading from his office. "Use that conference room," he said. "It's the one reserved for my rich clients."

"You honor us," said Seely. Grinning, he turned to Tim. "I knew this fella when his idea of getting a rich client was to chase an ambulance. Come on, Tim, let's go."

In the well-appointed room Seely seated himself on one side of a glass-topped table and motioned Tim to a chair on the other side. Seely lit a cigar while Tim tried to keep beads of perspiration from forming on his forehead. He finally had to mop it with a handkerchief.

"Relax," said Seely sympathetically. "The news isn't all bad."

The announcement helped some, though not enough

to take all the stiffness from Tim's muscles. Seely hastened to relieve Tim's suffering.

"You looked good yesterday. I liked what I saw, but as yet I don't consider you big-league material."

Tim's breath made a soft sound as he released it. He said, "Oh." His voice was dead and hollow.

"Now hold on," Seely said impatiently. "You haven't heard all I have to say."

Tim said, "Oh," again. There was more life to the sound of his voice this time.

Seely went on, "We don't toss contracts around like confetti. On the other hand, when we run across a likely prospect we try not to let him get away until we're sure he can't be of any use to us. That means you."

Tim's discouragement was evaporating fast. He edged forward in his chair.

"You'll get a fair tryout if you want to accept it on our terms," continued Seely. "To start with, we'll ask you to sign a contract, which is no assurance that you will ever play football for the Mohawks. We sew up your services for the club, of course, but the contract is primarily for your own protection. Clause fifteen, Injuries, provides that if you get hurt while playing football for us, we'll take care of you."

Tim nodded his approval.

"We'll pay your transportation to the training camp, and from the camp if you flunk out. You won't be on the payroll while you're there, but you'll get room and board and probably a small allowance for such things as laundry."

"What happens to the contract if I flunk out?" Tim asked.

"Clause six," said Seely. The scout picked up a contract. "It says here, and I quote, 'The Player represents and warrants that he is and will continue to be sufficiently highly skilled in all types of football team play, to play professional football of the caliber required by the League and by the Club, and that he is and will continue to be in excellent physical condition, and agrees to perform the services hereunder to the complete satisfaction of the Club and its Head Coach. If in the opinion of the Head Coach the Player does not maintain himself in excellent physical condition or fails at any time during the football seasons included in the term of this contract to demonstrate sufficient skill and capacity to play professional football of the caliber required by the League and by the Club, or if in the opinion of the Head Coach the Player's work or conduct in the performance of this contract is unsatisfactory as compared with the work and conduct of other members of the Club's squad of players, the Club shall have the right to terminate this contract upon written notice to the Player of such termination.' And there you have it."

"Takes a long time to get to the point, doesn't it?" said Tim dryly.

"Indeed it does," agreed Seely. "But the lawyers have to earn their pay."

"So if I flunk out I'm through," said Tim.

"Well, not necessarily. The club will release you on a waiver. That means other clubs are free to give you a contract. The chances are very slim, of course, if you don't last long at the camp. If you finish the entire training period before being released, it means you have something that may interest another club. There's also the chance that if you look good during training, the club will put you on the payroll. It doesn't begin for anybody until the start of the season. How does it sound?"

"It sounds great," said Tim.

Seely smiled. "That's fine, Tim, but it's only fair to warn you not to get your hopes too high. Pro football requires a certain type of man with certain qualities, and we can never be sure about a player until we put him through the wringer. Even college football is no more than a kindergarten compared to pro football, and I don't have to remind you that your football experience has been limited. You'll be surprised how little you actually know about the game."

"As bad as that?"

"Well, not quite," said Seely. "You've got a good passing arm, good balance, and you don't seem to rattle easily. You're a good runner, which is not a necessary attribute in a pro quarterback, but means that you could be used in other positions. There are a lot of college men, though, who are as good as you in those departments."

"I guess there are," conceded Tim, beginning to wonder why the scout was wasting time with him.

Seely promptly answered the question in Tim's mind. "The thing that really caught my interest, Tim, was instinct, *your* instinct I mean. You have a rare feeling for the game, and any player with that quality can be valuable, if, of course, his physical qualities can stand the test."

"And if they can't?" asked Tim, realizing too late that he had asked a stupid question.

Seely answered with a shrug. It was a good answer. The scout went on as if he had not been interrupted. "I watched you spot the Rams who were trying to put on a good show to impress me."

"You saw *that?*" asked Tim with genuine surprise.

Seely grinned, explaining, "That's what I'm paid for, son. I also watched the way you ran the team, even though you knew I had my eye on you. You had plenty of chances to try to be a hero, but instead of taking advantage of them, you called the plays you thought would be the most effective. I chalked it up to your credit because, from my angle, it meant that you kept your mind on the game and played to win."

"Well, thanks," said Tim.

"It's a little too early for thanks," reminded Seely.

"You've got a long, long way to go, Tim, if you decide to take my offer. You'd probably like to think it over."

"No sir," said Tim promptly. "I've been thinking it over since I heard you'd be watching the game. I'd like to try out for the Mohawks."

"Good. I'm glad," said Seely. "So let's sign the contracts. Here they are, one for you to keep, one for League headquarters, and one for the Mohawks. Do you want to read it?"

Tim grinned. "If it's all like the part you read to me, I'd be here until dark. I'll take your word that everything's okay. Where do I sign?"

"Right here." Seely indicated the place. "I sign on the line above as the 'authorized officer,' which I am."

Tim's signature was not as bold and clear as he would have liked it to be. The lines wobbled slightly from the trembling of his hand. In a happy daze he left the office, carrying his contract as if it were one of the Dead Sea scrolls. Bart Hogan met him in the office.

"Okay?" asked Hogan.

"A-okay!" said Tim. "I don't know how to thank you. If you hadn't. . . ."

"Knock it off," said Hogan gruffly. Then he added, "There may be some more good news waiting for you."

"What?"

"It's still a secret, but I've got a hunch the news will definitely be good."

Hogan was right. During a slack period at the filling

station that afternoon, Nick Jeffer's convertible pulled up at one of the pumps. When Tim approached the car, Nick's grin stretched almost to his ears. His voice was boisterous, "Hi, pal, meet your Mohawk buddy!"

"My *what?*" demanded Tim. Then the meaning hit him. "Have you flipped? Or are you telling me the truth?"

"The truth, so help me," Nick declared. "I'm in!"

Tim let the news sink in. When he could no longer doubt it, he let out a mighty whoop. Nick hopped from the car and they spent a few moments pounding each other's shoulders.

When the first wave of exuberance had died down, Tim asked, "How in thunder did you swing it?"

"Well, I didn't actually swing it by myself," admitted Nick. "I've got to give Dad credit. Of course, I *did* mention that Seely made me a proposition, the same one he made you, but I tried to pass it off as a joke. Maybe I'm poor at jokes, because Dad looked at me for a long time, and said, 'It's still in your system, isn't it?' I had to admit it was. He thought a while and told me, 'You'd better get it out. I think I can run the business in the meantime.' And that's the way it was."

"Is he sore at you?"

"No, just resigned. He's a great guy and he's smart. He knows I won't be worth a dime to him while I've got football on my mind. I honestly hate to do this to him, but I think we'll both be better off in the long run."

"I think so too."

"We can't let ourselves get rusty," Nick said practically. "I'll get a football and we'll keep working with it."

Another very practical point occurred to Tim a short time later, the matter of keeping himself in top-notch physical condition. His job in the filling station was active enough, but a man couldn't build up muscles by filling gas tanks and changing oil. With some reluctance he mentioned the problem to his boss, who, to Tim's relief, promptly agreed that he should look for another job.

"I'll hate to lose you, Tim, you know that. On the other hand, it's my civic duty to see that you're hard as nails when you reach the Mohawk camp. Any ideas?"

"Yes," acknowledged Tim. "Roy Bates, our left guard, owns his own farm, and I heard him say the other day that he's looking for a good hired hand. If he hasn't found one, I'll ask for the job."

Bates had not yet found the man he wanted. He seemed pleased that Tim would help him out. "I've got to warn you, Tim, that it's rough work for a man who's not accustomed to it—dawn to dark and all that sort of thing. Also, I can't afford to pay much."

"I'll take what you can afford. I'm not doing the work for money. I'm doing it to keep in shape."

"You'll keep in shape," said Bates with a grin. "That I can guarantee."

Roy Bates did not exaggerate. He set a rugged pace, which Tim gamely tried to match. Bates finally had to slow him down.

"Look, Tim," he explained, "farming is something like football. No coach would send you into a scrimmage before he got you ready for it. Ease up a bit. Don't try to do everything I do. Give your blisters a chance to catch up with you, and you'll be a farmer in no time."

Bates was right again. Tim slowed his pace, let his blisters heal, and soon became hardened to the strenuous life. He learned during the ordeal that he would never want to be a farmer, but he was proud of his ability to work side by side with Bates. He was also happy in the knowledge that he had never been stronger in his life, and that he was getting stronger every day. When he joined the Mohawks he would be in shape for football.

During the early stages of his farm work Tim was too tired at night to do proper work on the correspondence courses that would finish his high school requirements. As he hardened to the farm work he was able to complete them. It was a struggle in which he was sustained by the assurance that a genuine diploma would more than repay him for the effort and that he would be a proud and happy man when the diploma reached him through the mail.

When it finally came, he was disillusioned to find that he was neither proud nor happy. It was a letdown, a disappointment which he found hard to understand. He had worked hard for that diploma. He had earned it. Yet the elaborate document with scrolls and Latin words seemed somehow artificial, phony, as if he had obtained it illegally. He did not feel the satisfaction all his friends had known at graduation exercises, where diplomas had been presented to them openly for everyone to see and to applaud. So he was now an authentic high-school graduate. He had done it the hard way, yet he felt like a person who has joined a lively party through the back door.

Tim considered himself fortunate, however, to have other matters to occupy his mind. He worked hard through the winter, spring, and early months of summer. He and Nick Jeffer saw a lot of each other during that time. They had a common interest and a lot of things to talk about. They found time to practice, handling a football until it became a part of them.

Finally they both received letters from Matt Seely advising them that the big moment was at hand. They were to report at the Mohawk training camp in upper Maine on July fifteenth. Transportation money was enclosed. The *Greytown Morning Chronicle* grabbed eagerly at the news and made a big thing of it. *Local Boys to Join Mohawks* greeted readers from the front page of the paper.

"They're laying it on a little thick," Nick complained to Tim. "Sure, the local boys are going to join the Mohawks, but a lot of people must be wondering how long the local boys will stay there."

"I'm wondering too," admitted Tim.

The Cougar fans refused to settle for a newspaper send-off. Someone decided that a big farewell banquet was in order, and everyone fell in with the idea. To accommodate all the fans who wanted to attend, the banquet was held in the high-school gym, where an atmosphere of celebration overshadowed mediocre food. There were speeches, cheers, and everything that goes with farewell dinners. Tim was self-conscious through it all and glad when the festivities were over.

As they left the building, Nick looked worried. He said, "They've sure put us on the spot. How will we feel if we come slinking back here a few weeks from now? Me, I think I'll keep on going till I reach Brazil."

"You'll have company," said Tim.

Chapter Eleven

The letters that Tim and Nick received from Seely contained a short printed list of suggestions designed to smooth the path of recruits. Among these suggestions was a rather pointed one that the newcomers had better leave their automobiles at home in order to avoid the temptation to take side trips from the training area.

"Sounds like a prison camp," Nick grumbled. "I'll sure miss my little buggy."

"And I'll make a prophecy," said Tim. "You won't have time to miss it."

They made the trip by train, and Nick, to his surprise, enjoyed the new experience. "You may not believe this," he confided, "but I've never traveled this far before on one of these newfangled contraptions. They give you soft beds, keep you cool, and feed you well. Not bad at all."

They left Greytown in the afternoon and arrived in Bangor the following morning. Changing to a less pretentious train, they headed north through beautiful pine forests and past small, clean-looking lakes. There were other men on the train, quite a few of whom could only be football players.

"These guys look bright-eyed and hopeful," observed Nick. Then he added, "Just like us."

"We're probably the advance guard," said Tim. "I guess they want to get us squared away, so we won't clutter up the place when the real football players show."

"Could be," Nick agreed.

They reached their destination some three hours after leaving Bangor. The conductor called out, "Juniper Hill! Last stop!"

Looking from the window, Tim agreed, "What else could it be? There's no place else to stop. This looks like the end of civilization."

Nick finished counting and announced his findings. "Eight houses, a general store, and a garage. It looks as if the boys in camp won't be tempted to come into town for a wild time. Well, let's go."

They lifted their luggage, two bags apiece, from the rack above their head and joined the line of football players moving down the aisle. Once on the platform Tim shook the stiffness from his legs and took a deep breath of the crisp, pine-scented air. He dropped his suitcases on the platform in order to open his lungs wider for another breath, a breath he was not permitted to complete.

Someone behind Tim failed to stop. He banged into Tim's heavy suitcase, barked his shins, and, burdened with his own bags, made a game but futile effort to retain his balance. He managed a half spin before hitting the boards in a sitting, but ungraceful pose. He glared at Tim from that position, then came slowly to his feet, full of menace. He was about Tim's size and build, quite handsome in a narrow-featured way that crowded his eyes too close to his nose. Now his eyes had the color and quality of a blowtorch. His mood was not improved by a few guffaws from the men about him.

Tim hastened to apologize, "I'm sorry!"

"You'd better be, you stupid jerk! Did you think you had this platform all to yourself?"

The man moved closer, head thrust forward. Tim felt the short hairs bristling on his neck. He did not want to lose his temper, certainly not at this time or place, but the man's face and attitude had a strange effect on him, almost like a chemical reaction too powerful to control. The feeling was obviously mutual. Instead of retreating, as he knew he should have, Tim moved in with a sharp sense of exhilaration. Whatever might have happened was forestalled by a loud, authoritative voice.

"Knock it off! Where do you think you are? This is a football training camp, not a tryout for the Golden Gloves!"

The speaker was a man with size enough to enforce his orders. A sweat shirt stretched across his massive chest; a baseball cap clung to his round head. His face cried out for plastic surgery, but he wore the marks of old gridiron battles with dignity and pride.

Assured that the danger of a brawl had passed, he told the men about him, "I'm Monk Chedder, and there won't be any wisecracks on the last name. I'll be your coach, for a while at least."

He turned to Tim and the other rookie. Both were docile now, and both of them began to squirm under Monk's long, silent stare. He finally addressed the man who had run into Tim. "You're Luke Minty, aren't you?"

"Why yes," said Minty, regaining his assurance with the flattery of being recognized. His attitude suggested that a man of his importance would surely be forgiven a small transgression. He was wrong. Monk's expression did not soften.

"You're off to a bad start, Minty, a real bad start."

Luke Minty's face went red, but Monk had already turned to Tim. "And you, whatever your name is, are off to a bad start too. We don't like soreheads."

He turned and walked away, indifferent to Tim's name or football background, and began to herd the men into a waiting bus.

Tim, sitting beside Nick, said gloomily, "It sure is swell to make such a good impression right off the bat."

"It might be a break for you," said Nick. "Cheddar

will be sure to remember you next time he sees you, which is more than can be said for most of the guys in this bus. Naturally he'll remember Luke Minty. You know who Minty is, don't you?"

"It may sound stupid," Tim admitted, "but I never heard of him. I didn't read much football news while I was in the Navy."

"Luke's big time," Nick explained. "College big time, that is. He was picked for quarterback on most all-American teams, and he headed the draft list. The Mohawks had to shell out a fat bonus to get his name on a contract. He's hot stuff—valuable merchandise."

"He seems to know it, too," said Tim.

"It looks that way."

A twenty-minute ride brought them to the training camp. Tim looked about with interest, impressed with what he saw. The camp appeared to be a self-contained community made up of a variety of frame buildings with accommodations for the sixty to seventy players who would be on hand. There was no time for sight-seeing as Monk Cheddar hustled his charges to a small building that was obviously the camp office. The men were checked in and assigned to quarters.

There was nothing elaborate about the one-story dormitories, each of which could accommodate twenty men, two to a room. The rooms were small but airy, and the beds were sturdy enough to bear the weight of football players. There was a washroom at one end of the dormitory, and at the other end there was a lounge with comfortable chairs and a wide-screen television set. The men were permitted to choose their roommates, and Tim and Nick moved in together.

Monk Cheddar's final instructions were brief. "Take the rest of the day off. Make the most of it, because tomorrow you start work—and I mean work. Look around our fair city if you like. Don't wander off into the woods and get lost, and watch out for squirrels. Don't let them chase you. Stand right up to them."

Nick and Tim followed Monk's suggestion to look around the camp. The dining hall was no more than a large pavilion screened tightly on all sides. The kitchen was modern and spotless. Another building contained long lines of lockers, enough for all the players in the camp. There was a battery of showers at one end of the building. The equipment room and the training room were at the other end. The appointments of the training room were more than reassuring, including whirlpool baths and other devices to take care of injured men.

"Makes a fellow almost want to get himself banged up, doesn't it?" said Tim.

"Not quite," Nick disagreed. "Hey, look!" He pointed to a door leading off the training room. A sign *X-Ray* was lettered on the door. "That means the club doctor can make a fast diagnosis on the spot."

"A fine idea, but sort of gruesome," Tim observed.

"I was told the Mohawks have a small plane. It's mostly for the executives, but it can also be used to get an injured player to the hospital. They have a landing strip up here."

"You're in a cheerful mood today," said Tim. "But I agree with you that it's nice to know they're geared to take care of us."

Continuing their tour of inspection, they saw the pump house where water to supply the camp was pulled from a deep well. There was also a laundry building with equipment for dry-cleaning uniforms and even a small store supplied with such necessary items as toothpaste and razor blades.

Of even greater interest were the three football fields laid out so that their inner side lines formed a triangle. In the center of the triangle was a tower of metal tubing about thirty feet high. At the top, reached by a ladder, was a railed platform large enough to hold half a dozen men in comfort. Those of the coaches not active on the field could stand there and get an unobstructed view of all three gridirons.

"Whoever dreamed that up must have gone to a school for spies," said Tim. "It's an invasion of privacy."

"We'll be like germs under a microscope," Nick agreed. "When they pin us down with their binoculars they can even watch us breathe."

"Just the same, it's a good idea, and it'll really keep us on our toes. I'll guarantee there won't be any goofing off on any of *those* three football fields," said Tim.

The newcomers had their first look at the head coach, Mort Crowder, in the dining hall that evening. He was a square-built man with a mild manner, despite his reputation of being a high-speed dynamo, tough disciplinarian, and builder of great football teams. He made a short talk, which was a speech of welcome in its way, even though its contents chilled his listeners.

"You're in for a rough time," he began, "because statistics are not in your favor. They show that only one out of eight rookies ends up as a regular. You'll have to fight those statistics and a brand of football that will be entirely new to you.

"I'm not disparaging you college men with big reputations. You're fine football players or you wouldn't be here. The fact remains that you've merely scratched the surface of football technique, for no college can afford the training time we can. With us it's a full-time job. Unfortunately for you men, we can't afford much time to look you over, probably not as much time as we need. We don't claim to be infallible, and it's entirely possible we will discard some men whose actual potential we have not discovered. It's not a cheerful possibility, but it does exist."

He paused briefly to regard the sober, slightly alarmed faces turned in his direction. Then he smiled and went on, "That's the worst part. There is, of course, a silver lining. Those of you who are fortunate enough to make the regular squad will be playing football for money, and there are many instances where that money has contributed to a man's future successful life after he quits football.

"As soon as a rookie becomes a regular, he is covered by a ten-thousand-dollar life-insurance policy together with a major medical health insurance plan. There is also the Player Benefit Plan. Pro football is a booming sport, which should mean increases in the benefits of the plan. Right now, however, a five-year veteran may collect $437 a month for the rest of his life; a ten-year veteran, $656 monthly; and a fifteen-year veteran, $821 monthly. That, my friends, is not chicken feed. It should keep your spirits up and your game sharp. Any questions?"

Expressions around the table showed there were many questions trembling to be asked, but no one dared to quiz the formidable Mort Crowder.

The coach, reading many minds, said, "Okay, they'll probably last or get answered by themselves. I assume you men have met your head rookie coach, Monk Chedder." There were cautious nods. Crowder went on, "It's only fair to warn you not to regard Monk as your big daddy. The man's a beast, and my heart goes out to you."

There was a loud muttering from one of the tables.

"Did I hear something?" Crowder asked.

"You heard *me*," growled Monk. "Doesn't your heart go out to *me* a little?"

"No," said Crowder.

Monk sighed and said resignedly, "That's life."

Chapter Twelve

The Mohawk rookies started work next morning. Their first lesson came at dawn. A huge gong filled the dormitory with its violent clamor. Its noise jerked Tim's head off the pillow with the sleep-fogged notion that the place was burning down. He jumped out of bed and was promptly joined by Nick.

"Now *that*," observed Nick, "is what I call an alarm clock."

"I'm glad the Navy didn't think up one like that," growled Tim. "Maybe it's Monk Chedder's idea of a joke. So what happens now?"

The question was soon answered. Monk's voice roared, "Up and at 'em! Put on your shorts and shoes and come outside before I have to come and get you!"

Monk did not have to carry out his threat. The

rookies poured into the open as if the dormitories had been filled with tear gas. Monk lined them up for calisthenics. He gave them a hard workout, made somewhat easier by the invigorating crispness of the morning air. When the calisthenics were completed, he sent them for a mile jog around the football field. As they finished Monk watched each man carefully, checking for signs of poor condition or undue fatigue, and made notes on a sheet of paper fastened to a clipboard. Tim suspected that the notes were merely for fright value, because he doubted that Monk had had time to memorize the names and faces of the men. Nonetheless, Tim was glad that, thanks to the farm work, he was still reasonably fresh.

After a shower and a big breakfast the rookies were allowed to loaf a while, but not for long. The next call sent them to the training quarters where they lined up at the equipment counter to be issued uniforms. The outfits given to the rookies were obviously hand-me-downs. Tim's gear had seen considerable use, but it was clean and in good repair. There was a lot of wear still left in it, and Tim was satisfied.

The rookies were told to help themselves to any locker not already claimed by one of the regulars. Some of the names on the lockers were famous, names that would go down in pro football history. Other names, even though they might not be known to posterity, belonged to men who had a firm grip on their Mohawk jobs. Tim and Nick tactfully passed up lockers near those bearing famous names, feeling it would not be wise to attempt to mingle with the great this early. They finally chose a pair of empty lockers adjoining one marked *B. B. Meeker.*

"That must be Bobo Meeker," Nick speculated. "He was a rookie last year, one of the best offensive linemen in the league. I guess we can park here without anyone accusing us of social climbing."

Tim placed his gear on the floor while he opened the locker. He would be getting into the uniform at once for the morning workout, so there was no point in stowing it away. As he took off his shirt and was hanging it in the locker, he heard a sound behind him. He turned and found his football gear scattered over the floor. The person who had kicked it was Luke Minty. Luke pretended to be angry, but he looked pleased.

"So it's *you* again!" Luke rasped. "Can't you *ever* find a place to put your stuff except under somebody's feet?"

Tim held his temper, slightly frightened by the ease with which it rose against Minty.

"Look at it this way," Tim suggested. "Not every-body's feet are as big and clumsy as yours seem to be."

The pleased look left Luke's face. "Don't bug me," he warned.

"Well now," Tim went on reasonably, "if I was wrong about your big clumsy feet, then you must have kicked my stuff on purpose."

Luke's voice got louder. "How could I see your stuff over this pile of junk I'm carrying? Tell me that, wise guy! Am I supposed to carry a periscope?"

Tim had no chance to answer. Monk Chedder barged upon the scene. "Aha!" he said, his voice ominously soft. "I see you little lovebirds are at it again. Who started it this time?"

Neither man claimed the distinction.

Monk turned to Luke. "Nice football players don't kick another man's good expensive equipment around on the floor."

Luke, not knowing how much of the previous action Monk had seen, must have decided that a surprise attack was better than retreat. It was a poor decision, not improved by Luke's rising anger.

"Good expensive equipment," Luke repeated with heavy sarcasm. "This stuff is junk, and you know it! It's lousy secondhand junk! What do you think we are, a bunch of sandlotters?"

Tim winced, but no one noticed. Nick grinned, but no one noticed that either. The other rookies were at full attention now, watching with interest while Monk pondered his next move. It was a masterpiece.

"No, Minty," Monk conceded, "I don't think that. I know you men all have good football backgrounds or you wouldn't be here. The thing that did slip my mind is that you're so much better than the rest, and there's no reason why we should treat you like a common rookie. Now you take that junk back to the equipment room, and I'll see that you get another outfit—all brand-new."

Monk waited a moment for his words to sink in. Some of the color left Luke's face as the implication of Monk's offer became clear. Luke had blundered into a bad trap and had sense enough to know it. He did not want to be so completely set apart from the other men. He would have to work closely with them for weeks to come, and, if they so wished, they could make him look like a third-string quarterback.

Luke muttered, "I'll wear these."

Before he turned away, he shot a glance at Tim. It said, unreasonably, "You got me into this mess, and I won't forget it."

Tim expected a few words of caustic advice from Monk, but the coach turned and walked away with the air of a man who has done his good deed for the day.

The rookies worked out in the morning and again in the afternoon. There was no contact work in the early stages of training, merely a general assessment of each man's ability and physical condition. Tim passed, kicked, and ran a few simple signals. It was nice to be with a group of football players once more. It was also nice, but slightly frightening, to sense the high caliber of the men. Playing with hand-picked talent was a new experience, and he wondered if his own game would stand up to theirs.

The wake-up gong next morning had its echo in loud pitiful groans as the rookies forced their aching muscles out of bed. Tim was again glad that farm work had spared him the agony that was all around him. Calisthenics brought out painful grunts, but at breakfast no one's appetite seemed dulled. The men ate like starving refugees, and another day was under way.

Most of the regulars showed up at camp the following day, and Tim had his first chance to meet the man whose locker adjoined his. Tim and Nick were suiting up for morning practice when B. B. Meeker arrived. He was huge. It was hard for Tim to mind his manners and not stare at the giant, whom Tim judged to be about six and a half feet tall and to weigh in the vicinity of three hundred pounds, a formidable hunk of human flesh, solid and well-proportioned.

Tim was minding his own business when a soft voice, anything but formidable, said, "Hello."

Tim turned and met a pair of mild blue eyes set in a pleasant, guileless face. Meeker's smile was hesitant, almost apologetic for his towering size that made other men look small. "Hello," Tim answered Meeker's greeting.

"I'm Bogart Boliver Meeker," the big man introduced himself. "They've shortened it to Bobo."

"I'm Tim Barlow, and this is Nick Jeffer."

"Nick Jeffer," Bobo repeated, pleased. "I've heard of you. You're getting up here late."

Nick nodded. "Family pressure. I finally wore them down."

Bobo turned to Tim and asked, "What's your school, Tim?"

Tim tried to keep the stiffness from his face as he replied, "High school—third year. They found me on a sandlot."

"No kidding!" Bobo said. "Boy, that's *something!*"

Tim warmed immediately to him. There was no hint of criticism in Bobo's voice, no assumption of superiority, merely wonder and respect for a man who had made his first long stride toward big-league football from such an unlikely base.

Bobo let the subject drop as if it had been settled to his satisfaction. He warned, "They make it tough for rookies, but it's got to be that way to weed out the ones they don't want. They're fair about it, though, as fair as they can be. I know, because I was a rookie last year. I also picked up a few pointers that could be helpful to new men. I'll pass them on to you boys now and then if you want me to."

"You bet we do," said Tim.

A strange thing happened then. Bobo nodded pleasantly, then seemed to wipe both Tim and Nick completely from his mind. He seemed, in fact, to wipe everything around him from his consciousness. There was nothing personal about it, nothing rude. It was quite as if he had gone into a trance. His football gear was still piled up on the floor. He left it there while he sat down on a bench and stared into his empty locker. He kept on staring while Tim and Nick pulled on their football togs and shot occasional uneasy glances at the motionless Bobo. Tim began to wonder seriously if something should be done about his condition. He was glad when Monk Chedder showed up to relieve him of the responsibility. He stopped behind Bobo and diagnosed the symptoms properly. He slapped Bobo smartly on the shoulder.

"Okay, Bobo! Up and at 'em!"

Bobo grunted, then shook his head as if clearing it of fog. He turned a thoroughly normal grin on Monk and said, "Thanks, Coach."

Tim and Nick were suited up by that time. They exchanged puzzled glances and headed for the field. Monk joined them. Once outside, Monk said, "So long as your lockers are so close together, I guess I'd better tell you something about Bobo."

"Is—is something wrong with him?" asked Tim.

"Depends on how you look at it," said Monk, amused. "It's not quite fair to call him an oddball. Egghead is a better word."

"*Him?* An egghead?" demanded Nick. "I pegged him for a real nice guy, but hardly a big brain."

"You pegged him wrong," said Monk. "He has a master's degree in architecture and is working for a Ph.D.

From what I hear he's a real whiz. I understand he's been offered some good jobs with architectural firms, but he wants to teach instead. He's earning money at football so he can study for a while in Europe."

"He had me worried in the locker room," said Tim. "Does he have those spells often?"

"Now and then," said Monk. "When he gets that blank look, he's working out some problem in his head. At times, he's as absentminded as the professors you read about."

"Does it ever happen during a game?" Nick asked.

"In a way it does," said Monk. "But at those times he has nothing but football on the brain. I've never known a player with such complete concentration. When the other team has the ball and Bobo's on the bench, his mind snaps up anything connected with football, but if you showed him a newspaper with a headline saying that the Empire State Building had collapsed, it might not even register on him."

"I like the guy," said Tim.

Monk nodded. "Everybody does. And we wish we had a dozen linemen just like Bobo."

Chapter Thirteen

The training season moved into high gear with the arrival of the regulars, some of whom knew well enough their jobs were not secure while a bunch of hungry rookies were fighting to replace them. No one, rookie or old-timer, dared to loaf.

The threat of three deadlines hung above the men like the sword of Damocles, holding particular menace for the rookies. League rules decreed that the cumbersome squad of sixty or more men be cut to forty-five three weeks before the opening of the season. Two weeks before the season's start, two more men had to be eliminated to bring the total down to forty-three. A week later three more men were dropped, reducing the club to its legal strength of forty.

During training hours, the constant action on and

about the three gridirons might have looked like an aimless scramble. It was far from that. Beneath the whole
operation was the cool efficiency of a precise machine.
Every man knew what he was doing and every coach
knew what each man under him was doing, either on the
field, in the tackling pits, or on the fiendish rushing racks
designed to torture linemen.

Dominating the whole scene was the observation
tower where Mort Crowder spent a lot of time, sweeping
the area with his binoculars and missing very little. His
method of communicating with the coaches was not sub-
tle. A loudspeaker blared forth when he wished to make a
comment. All comments were constructive; all were
pointed; few were flattering.

Tim fell into the routine with an ease he found encouraging. His love of football made the life seem almost
normal, except for the constant tension and uncertainty.
The days slid by with alarming speed, each one bringing
him a step closer to the first deadline, and as that day
approached the nerves of all the rookies frayed.

Tim's acceptance of the routine was about the only
thing he found encouraging. The program was impersonal
to a point that no rookie knew exactly where he stood or
what progress he was making. Yet Tim was able to accept
the logic of the system. At this stage of training, a coach
should not show favoritism to any single man. All rookies
must be considered equal and accorded an equal chance,

and Tim had to concede that Monk was doing a fine job. He was also a fine coach, thorough, exacting, yet surprisingly patient. He was the right man for the job.

Tim's uncertainty about his own progress was founded on circumstance. He was assigned such a variety of positions that he had no way of being sure what spot, if any, the coaches had in mind for him. They used him in the backfield as a blocking back, as a wingback, and even as a halfback. They tried him at offensive end and at defensive end. They gave him a whirl at cornerback, that vital, lonesome spot, requiring speed, weight, guts, and the instinct to sense a pass or an end run. He had his turn on the suicide squad, the kickoff receiving unit, whose members are expected to risk life and limb at full speed ahead.

He was permitted an occasional turn at quarterback, where he could run the team to suit himself and where he could limber up his passing arm. These turns, though welcome, were scarcely satisfactory because of the limited time to study the defense.

So far as Tim could tell, he discharged the varied duties reasonably well. There was no way of knowing, though, how Monk and the other coaches felt about him. Their mental and written notes were shared only among themselves. Tim hoped that his sessions at quarterback had met with approval. He gleaned a wisp of satisfaction from the fact that Luke Minty, a man with an established reputation as a quarterback, was receiving the same general treatment. When Tim took time to give his chances serious thought, however, his confidence chilled.

Calm reasoning told him that the Mohawks needed a rookie quarterback about as much as they needed a giraffe. To start with, they had one of the best quarterbacks in the league, Jerry Muller. Muller, to be sure, was thirty-seven, an old man in pro ranks, but he had attained his present peak through long experience and with the help of a cast-iron constitution. He was not much of a runner, but his pinpoint passing was lethal and his football brains were incredibly canny. He ran the team in an unhurried, steady way, and he was always boss.

Behind Muller was another quarterback, Buck Fisher. Three years out of college, Fisher ran the team with a flamboyant, flashy style in contrast to Muller's calm efficiency. Muller could get more out of a team than Fisher in the long haul, but the younger man was effective as an occasional replacement. He brought a change of pace that his own team had learned to accept, but that opponents found confusing.

Another man, Jiggs Clemment, could be used in an emergency. Clemment was a five-year veteran, a fine ball handler and a player of sound judgment. He was the only man, according to Tim's reasoning, who might possibly be replaced, and Tim was far from sure that his own talents were sufficient to move him into Clemment's spot. If such a change were made, it seemed more likely that Luke

Minty would get the call, a thought that depressed Tim thoroughly.

Luke also must have figured he had a chance at Clemment's job. His efforts all seemed pointed in that direction. He was playing it smart, for which Tim had to give him credit. Realizing that he'd made a big fool of himself before the other rookies in the locker room, Luke started to rebuild his fences, making friends in an apologetic, unassuming way that appeared to be effective even though it seemed entirely out of character.

Noticeably, Luke's goodwill drive did not include Tim Barlow. He avoided Tim in a manner that suggested he could not trust his temper in Tim's presence. It suggested, too, that a high school dropout, a sandlot player, was too unimportant to be noticed by an all-American. The arrangement suited Tim, but he did not kid himself that Luke's indifference toward him was a good omen. Luke was the sort of man who would not let a grudge die.

Nick's comment on Luke's campaign was brief. "It makes me sick," he said.

"He's getting by with it," Tim pointed out.

"I'm afraid he is," admitted Nick.

"He's a football player, too," said Tim reluctantly. "They've shifted him around as much as they have me, and he fills every spot well. He's a great passer and he handles the ball like a magician. I hope my chance to make the grade doesn't depend on a choice between Luke and me."

"You're as good as he is," Nick declared. "In my book, you're better."

"Thanks, pal. But assuming I *am* as good as Luke, what chance will I have against a bonus player? The club's got to protect its investment, and I can't blame it for that."

"Quit hanging crepe. You're not dead yet. Your chances are as good as mine."

Tim shook his head. "You're in. I'm sure of it. They've quit shifting you around and spotted you at end. There's not a rookie in the same class with you. Also, if the club has a weakness, it's at the ends. They can use you and I'm glad."

"Thanks, but I'd be a chump to count on it until after the Rookie Bowl. Anything could happen there."

Mention of the Rookie Bowl sent a chill down Tim's spine. All rookies, as well as several so-called regulars whose jobs were hanging by a thread, were worried about the Rookie Bowl. Though it received no official recognition from the club, it was tacitly conceded to be the final test that would separate the hopefuls from the chosen. The game would be the climax of training-camp activities and coincide with the first drastic cut three weeks before the opening of the season.

The coaches would have to make decisions at that time. Some of the decisions would be easy; others would be hard and probably painful. They would have to reduce the squad to forty-five men, always facing the possibility that some of the decisions might be wrong. Having studied the men carefully for a month, however, they would not make many errors.

By game time the coaches would undoubtedly have arrived at most of their selections. The borderline cases would be given a final chance to parade their talent in the Rookie Bowl. The men in the game would, for the most part, be desperate and uncertain, a condition that would put them under heavy pressure and possibly reveal strengths or weaknesses the coaches had missed so far. Those players who stayed on the bench would know that their fate had been decided one way or another.

Tim got little sleep the night before the Rookie Bowl. He tossed about trying not to disturb Nick. His concern was wasted.

Nick finally said, "Me, too. I can't sleep."

"I guess I'm scared," said Tim. "Scared stiff. I can't relax."

"I know," said Nick. "Making the team means a lot to me, but it's bound to mean a whole lot more to you."

They spoke softly, aware that the walls of their room were thin, aware, too, that they were not the only wakeful rookies in the dormitory.

After a moment's silence Tim agreed, "I'm afraid it means *too* much to me. I realize I shouldn't attach so much importance to getting on the team, but it's almost as if I were facing my last big chance."

"That's nonsense."

"I know. I can't help feeling that way, though. I've finally decided that a college education is terribly important. Maybe it's because I've been thrown in with so many college men here in camp and realize they all have their education to fall back on if they get sent home. If I don't make the grade I'm right back where I started, a twenty-three year old guy with a strong back and a high-school diploma from a correspondence school. Sounds grim, doesn't it?"

"You make it sound that way."

"Yes, I suppose I *am* looking on the dark side, but the bright side is so very bright that I'm almost scared to look at it. If the club thinks I'm good enough to use, even for a few years, it means I will have the money and the time to get that college sheepskin during the months I'm not playing football. I might even be lucky enough to decide on what sort of an education I really want. The game tomorrow may decide my whole future one way or another."

"It could," Nick admitted, "particularly if that's the way you feel about it. But you've got to remember that although this game may be the first big step, it's not the final one. The club will have three more weeks to decide whether or not they want to keep on any of us."

Tim began to feel better, surprised that the simple business of talking about his worries could make the difference. The knots in his nerves gradually untied, and his sleep, though not completely sound, was adequate.

His tension began to mount again in the morning. The men were not awakened by the gong, a change in the routine that in itself was disturbing. It advertised the fact that the day was indeed very special. The gladiators were being treated with unaccustomed kindness before they appeared in the arena.

Tim was not alone in his battle against quivering nerves. The symptoms were on all sides of him, developing like an epidemic. Rookies, and some of the regulars as well, excused from their usual morning exercise were wandering aimlessly about the place with glassy eyes and the tendency to jump at unfamiliar sounds. All were grateful, despite the grim significance of the moment, when they were permitted to suit up and report to the field.

Tim, as well as most of the others, was completely in the dark as to what position, if any, he would play in the coming game. The added bit of uncertainty did not improve his nerves. He stood around with the rest while the coaches held a final conference over their battle plans. The players would be divided into two squads, the Blue and the Green. Light, tear-away jerseys of these colors would be worn over their regular uniforms. When the jerseys were distributed, Tim was issued a blue one and sent to the Blues' bench on the far side of the field.

The big moment finally came when the names of the

starting teams were read. Monk Chedder dropped them
into the heavy silence. Tim listened with a tautness that
developed into misery as his name was not mentioned. He
had been chosen neither for offense nor for defense. He did
not even receive the doubtful honor of being selected for
the suicide squad. He took a place on the bench, trying
hard not to let his shoulders sag.

As the game got under way, he tried to reason with
himself. There were two ways of looking at the situation.
He could, if he chose, assume that his performance during
the past month had been impressive, that the coaches did
not need to learn more about him, that he pleased them
just as he was. On the other hand, maybe they had seen
all they cared to see of him in action. Maybe they knew
they couldn't use him. Maybe he would warm the bench
for the remainder of the day.

It was no boost to his morale when Luke Minty
pranced onto the field after the kickoff to take over at
quarterback for the attacking Green team. The only bright
spot in the picture was that Nick Jeffer also joined that
squad in the position where he rightly belonged, at end.
Despite his own sharp disappointment, Tim was sincerely
pleased that Nick would have this chance. He did not
doubt that Nick would make it.

Tim watched the Green team start its attack. He did
not care, at this point, whether the Greens won or lost.
Victory was not the purpose of this game. It was merely

a display of individual performances with each man fighting his own battle in the hope that he, rather than the
team, would be the winner.

Tim told himself there was no actual reason why he
should watch the game except that it was there to watch,
and it came as a surprise that his attention, although academic, remained fixed on the play. He simply could not
ignore football in any form. So he watched the play involuntarily, seeing the action in quick, photographic
flashes that registered clearly on his mind and were retained.

He saw what he expected to see, fine individual
performances, which, taken as a whole, lacked the close,
effective coordination of men fighting for a common cause
and accustomed to each other's style of play. He could not
help but wonder how much the coaches were learning
from their study of the play, but he decided they were
learning plenty. It was unlikely their experienced eyes
missed much on the field. If they did miss anything they
were sure to spot it later in the film of the game. The
camera was grinding relentlessly away on top of the observation tower.

Tim watched Luke move the Green team up the field.
At times Luke called for plays that Tim would not have
chosen, yet he had to admit that Luke was running the
team well. His ball handling behind the line was excellent
and deceptive. His passing was sound for the most part,

even though it might have lacked some of its effectiveness without the brilliant help of Nick Jeffer, who ran fine pass patterns and came up with some terrific catches.

Tim was critical of one aspect of Luke's game. Luke was a good ball carrier with speed, shiftiness, and judgment, but he seemed to be deliberately manufacturing opportunities to run with the ball. On option plays he swung wide for a pass and delayed a small fraction of a second until his eligible receivers were covered. By then, of course, he had run with the ball himself, just as he had planned to. Usually, he gained ground.

Tim could not believe the coaches were being fooled by Luke's heroics, and if the coaches were *not* fooled, he reasoned that Luke was making a mistake. Tim was aware that a fine running quarterback was an asset to a pro team, but only in an emergency or for a surprise attack. The quarterback option, pass or run, was a great weapon for a college team. Used sparingly, it was also good for a pro team. However, a first-string pro quarterback was much too valuable to risk on running plays where the opposition can put him out of action. A quarterback got hit more than enough behind the line. Why gamble with disaster in the open field? Tim knew better, and Luke Minty should have known too.

Chapter Fourteen

Whatever Tim's criticisms, Luke led the Green team to a touchdown. Just how far he would have led the team against seasoned opposition was hard to say. Nevertheless, a touchdown was a touchdown, and Tim had to give Luke credit for accomplishing the job. He was not impressed, however, by Luke's smug expression as he jogged off the field. His attitude seemed to say, "If that's all there is to pro football, brother, I've got it made!"

The Blue suicide squad and the Green kickoff unit went onto the field. Tim stayed on the bench. When the kickoff runback had been downed, the Blue offensive unit and the Green defensive players got the call. The Blues were being quarterbacked by the third stringer, Jiggs Clemment. His job, according to rookie gossip, was not too secure, and it almost looked as if he were in the game to prove his worth against the flashy all-American, Luke Minty.

Clemment carried the Blues to a pair of first downs, yet, according to Tim's observations, his performance was merely adequate. Tim knew that there were many things he might have missed, factors over which the quarterback had no control. Even so he felt a little sorry for Jiggs Clemment.

When the Blues gave up the ball, Luke had another chance to do his stuff. He hurried onto the field with confidence in every move, determined to carry on where he'd left off. It did not quite work out that way. He faced a defense that was virtually the same—with two exceptions. A veteran cornerback and a veteran safety man had come into the game, and the change made a tremendous difference in the Greens' attack. An offensive change appeared to weaken the Green team still more. Nick Jeffer was no longer at right end. The new set of conditions recommended that Luke revise his strategy, something he was unable to do in the short time allowed him. The first series of downs netted only six yards and the Greens were forced to kick on the fourth down. There was nothing cocky about Luke when he came off the field now. There was nothing cowed about him either. He looked thoughtful and no less determined.

Tim recognized that this game was set apart from others by a feature that made the job of the offensive players, particularly the job of the quarterback, considerably harder. The teams had been hastily drilled, for the coaches had been allowed but two days to build their squads, and so the signals had to be simple, almost rudimentary. In that length of time, no team could master the complex maze of plays so essential to the sort of competition a pro team has to face.

The coaches would undoubtedly be keeping a close eye on the quarterback to determine what use he could make of his team's limited maneuverability. They would watch the other offensive players as well. The defensive team would come in for its share of scrutiny. How effectively could the defenders take advantage of a situation definitely in their favor?

When the ball changed hands, Luke Minty got the call again. Obviously he was to be given every chance to show what he could do. He turned in a good performance during the remainder of the period and was helped when the veteran Blue linebackers were replaced by men of less experience. His passes were accurate enough, and the percentage of completions was high when Nick Jeffer was in the game.

Luke restricted his own running, either voluntarily or on orders from the bench. He used it as a surprise weapon, rather than a conventional one, and it was more effective that way. Best of all, he retained his poise, a great asset in a quarterback. Tim admitted to himself, without much satisfaction, that Luke was putting on a first-rate show. Tim envied him the chance to show what he could do.

As the game went on Tim's spirits sank. He had been watching the play, absorbing information as he always did, but it began to look as if the Mohawk brains had passed him up. They had him on the bench and would probably keep him there. His morale had sunk so low that the summons, when it came, caught him unprepared.

He heard Monk's voice bark, "Barlow!"

Tim came half off the bench. "Huh?"

"On your feet!" snapped Monk. "Take over the right cornerback!"

Tim needed no more urging. He came off the bench as if stung by a hornet, grabbed his helmet, then hesitated briefly to hear if Monk had instructions to send in. He had none, and Tim sprinted onto the field, loving the feel of turf beneath his cleats. The promise of impending action cleared his head and his brain began to function.

Tim wasted no regret on the decision to put him in at cornerback. He would have preferred to be at quarterback, of course, but any spot at all was preferable to sitting on the bench. The job assigned to him was one of the toughest on the field, and he had a good idea why he was being sent there. Too many of Luke's successful passes had been completed in that area.

Judging from his experience during practice as a cornerback, Tim was mildly flattered to be chosen for the position, a lonesome spot and one of huge responsibility. A cornerback had to have weight enough and guts enough to stop the charge of a 225-pound back. He had to have the speed, judgment, and maneuverability to cover either the spread end or the flanker back, man to man, on pass plays. Pass coverage was the roughest part of the assignment, because ends and flankers were always men with talent in running patterns and receiving passes.

When Tim came into the game, the Greens had the ball on their own thirty-six-yard line, first down. Luke stared at Tim in a calculating way that carried its own message. Tim did not claim to be a mind reader, but there was small chance for him to miss the intent of Luke's stare. It seemed almost as if this were the moment Luke had waited for. Tim was certain Luke would try to run through his position immediately, and he decided to gamble on that hunch.

The Greens came out of the huddle into a spread formation. Tim spotted himself opposite the wide left end, who, when the ball was snapped, scurried upfield as an eligible receiver. Quickly faking as if to follow, Tim then whirled back toward the scrimmage line. A quick glance showed that one of the alert safeties, Toby Clark, had taken over the job of covering the end, leaving Tim to his own business near the line.

There was a lot of action packed into a few violent seconds. While Luke was swinging wide to fake a pass, his blockers, a guard and a pair of backs, moved out ahead of him with the grim purpose of trampling the cornerback into the dirt.

Tim delayed his charge for an instant, permitting the pattern of the play to form clearly in his mind. He got some help from his right linebacker, who moved in to stop the lead blocker. Two men were left between Tim and Luke, who was holding down his speed until Tim was eliminated from the play. Tim made his flash decision when he noted that the two backs were coming at him too close together. Instead of spacing their attack, giving the second man a chance in case the first one missed, they tried to beat each other to the kill.

They were making a tactical mistake, according to Tim's reasoning. Two men, acting as a unit, might possibly behave like one under proper provocation. Tim tested the theory by a quick fake to the right. The two Greens, knowing that Tim could see the runner and that they could not, grabbed the bait. They assumed that Luke was leaving his blockers for a swift dash to the left. Their assumption was all wrong, as Tim had hoped it would be.

Both backs swerved to the left, taking the ball carrier by surprise. Luke, though a fast man on his feet, was not quite fast enough. He was a fraction of a second late in charting a new course, and during that brief tick of time Tim recovered balance from his fake and had a clear shot at Luke. He drove in hard, catching Luke an instant before he had a chance to change direction. He smashed a shoulder into Luke's belly, heard a painful grunt, and then the alarm call, "Ball! Ball! Ball!" Tim's tackle had separated Luke from the ball. There was the usual wild scramble for the pigskin, and one of Tim's teammates came up with it.

When Tim and Luke untangled and got off the ground, Luke's face was stiff with the shock of what had happened to him. The fumble and loss of the ball was a rookie's nightmare. Tim might even have felt sorry for him, but the emotion never developed. Luke turned on Tim, and he took a hasty backward step in the honest belief that Luke was about to throw a punch. Luke, however, did not compound his fumble by starting a slugfest. He controlled himself with difficulty, then headed for the side line to make way for the attacking unit.

Tim, too, went reluctantly to the bench. He was pleased, of course, that his brief stint at cornerback had been successful, even a bit spectacular, but it seemed unfair that his appearance on the field had been cut so short. One play, and that was it. He could not even be sure he would have another chance. The odds were in his favor, but nothing was certain at this stage. The highly specialized nature of pro football was a hardship on a person who loved the complete game and would choose to play for sixty minutes if permitted.

The game was played today by a group of trained technicians, men who sat restlessly on the bench until their own particular talent was required on the field. When that time came they fit into the machine like cogs, playing the positions they had been trained for. Tim resented the system, and yet could understand that it had advantages. A man could concentrate his entire energy on the job assigned to him and, if successful, could achieve both fame and fortune.

Tim's musings were interrupted sooner than he had expected. On the second play from scrimmage another rookie disgraced himself by fumbling the ball and seeing it go over to the other team. Hearing no order to the contrary, Tim jumped off the bench with the Blue defensive team and started for the field. By the time he had crossed the side line he knew he was safe. He noted with satisfaction that Luke was coming in again with the Green offensive unit. Nick also came in with the Greens, but he was on the right end so there was small chance that he and Tim would have contact on a play. If Tim had to make a good showing for himself, he would rather it not be at Nick's expense, and he was sure that Nick would prefer to look good against someone other than Tim Barlow.

A veteran replacement had been sent in again as left cornerback to keep an eye on Nick, a move that seemed planned to further the duel between Luke and Tim. With an able man covering Nick Jeffer, Luke would have to assume that the right side of the Blue line, with Tim Barlow at cornerback, would be more vulnerable to deep passes and to sideline passes. Tim guessed that his position would be a frequent point of attack.

Luke did not wait long to confirm Tim's guess. With the ball on the Blue forty-eight-yard line centered between the side lines, the Greens were in a fine position for attack. Luke spread his left end, sent a flanker to the right, then tried to foul up the Blue defense with a draw play. He almost got away with it, but the middle linebacker, though drawn briefly out of position, managed to scramble back in time to down the Green fullback after a three-yard gain.

On the second down Luke brought his men up to the line in the same formation. After the snap, the play broke to the left, and Tim found himself again on the hot spot. Luke swung wide with the ball cocked as if to pass. The left end, Grundy, had already passed Tim on his way to the receiving area, and Handy, the left half, had also headed upfield to a position from which he could cut either right or left. Tim dared not commit himself at once. He had to waste another instant trying to solve the pattern of the play, well aware that Luke would welcome a second chance to run the ball through his position. If he left a receiver uncovered, however, Luke could easily make a fool of him.

A swift glance told him that his right safety had taken on the job of covering Handy, which was all to the good. Another glance showed him that both his right linebacker and the middle linebacker had angled through for a shot at Luke in case he decided to run with the ball. They were forcing Luke hard, and it was almost certain that Luke would have to get rid of the ball or eat it.

Tim whirled then and started after the left end, Grundy, who by this time had a lead of several yards. Grundy was fast, but Tim knew his own speed was just a trifle better. His brain began to click then, bringing up small items that had been tucked away subconsciously, bits of football information that had the tendency to pop out of storage when he needed them.

Grundy was a fine receiver, almost surefire when he got his hands on the ball. Tim recalled, however, that Grundy still had things to learn about the art of faking. He would swerve to the right or left as he was supposed to in order to confuse a defender, but his left swerve was invariably an awkward, lunging effort, which seldom changed his course in that direction. When he faked this time toward the left side line, Tim was ninety percent certain that Grundy was indeed faking and that a side-line pass was not in the cards. Tim's filing system also came up with the fact that Grundy, when he turned and saw the pass coming at him, always raised his hands in the direction of the ball a fraction of a second too soon, thereby giving his defender a useful bit of information.

Grundy's fake to the left slowed him down. The gap between the pair closed when Tim failed to fall for the deception. When Grundy looked across his shoulder and swerved right, Tim knew the change of direction was authentic, so he swerved in that direction too. Grundy jammed on the brakes and reached for the ball, telling Tim where the ball was coming so that he could hold off for an instant longer before making his own turn and reach.

Tim timed his move on the dot. The pass was a bullet, coming too hard for Tim to risk an interception. If the ball got through his hands it would probably end up in Grundy's, and Grundy would be on his way to a touchdown. The gamble was too great, even for the sake of becoming a hero, so Tim let his common sense override temptation. He batted the ball down with both hands flat and open to be sure he did the job. The pass was incomplete, and when Tim came back to the scrimmage line, Luke regarded him without affection.

Faced with third down and seven, it was a safe bet that Luke would try the air again, so the defensive signal called for an all-out blitz to put the clamps on Luke before he could get rid of the ball. The Blue defense setup indicated that a blitz was on its way, and the defenders assumed that Luke was expecting it and would call his play with the blitz in mind. The defense could rule out a long pass if the blitzers did their job. A receiver would not have time to get very far beyond the scrimmage line. A line play or a short pass across the line were the best possibilities.

The play turned out to be the latter, even though the Blue linebackers were set up to defend against it. Nick

Jeffer was playing a tight end with a flanker out beyond him. Either of these men, or the spread left end, could cut in behind the line for the short pass. Nick got the call. He avoided a brush block by a blitzer and cut in fast.

The man assigned to Nick had him thoroughly covered, or at least he thought he did. Luke's hurried pass was high, as it should have been to avoid the reach of the linemen. Both Nick and the defender went into the air for it, but Nick's leap was higher and more closely timed. The ball smacked into his hands and stayed there. The defender made a frantic grab at him, but Nick twisted free with the agility of a cat, came back to earth, regained balance, and started for pay dirt.

Tim, meanwhile, knowing the pass would have to be a short one, had let the Green left end go galloping up the field. Tim moved in toward the action, noting that his right linebacker would be of no help. He had been pulled out of position by the threat of a Green halfback who had also cut toward the short-pass receiving zone.

Tim got away to a sprinting start. There was no loyalty in his heart, merely football instinct, as he saw his close friend gathering speed toward the end zone. Tim's small advantage lay in the fact that he had not had to regain balance after catching a pass. It was close figuring, but he thought his advantage could be measured by about one stride.

When Nick saw Tim coming at him, he must have

figured the same way. He knew their speeds were approximately the same and that at this point he would have no chance to outrun Tim. He did the next best thing. He came directly in at Tim and tried to fend him off with a straight-arm. It almost worked. Nick topped Tim's charge with a flat hand against his shoulder pads, but before Tim took a nose dive to the turf, he snaked out a long arm and got a partial grip on Nick's ankle. Nick managed to shake loose from the grip, but the effort cost him precious balance. He staggered forward for a few steps, unable to regain it. His knee came in contact with the ground, and the referee's whistle sounded. The ball was down.

Nick asked, "Is that the way to treat a friend? Nice work, Tim."

"You did all right yourself," said Tim. "That was a great catch, and you came through with a first down. Besides," he added, flexing the shoulder that had been temporarily numbed by Nick's straight-arm, "you weren't very friendly either."

Chapter Fifteen

Tim lined up for the next play feeling good about the one before. He had undoubtedly saved a touchdown by alert defensive work, and, at the same time, had not detracted from Nick's fine performance. Both men had appeared to good advantage. Tim hoped the play had been duly noted by the coaches.

Nick's run had moved the ball to the Blue thirty-five-yard line. Luke strode from the huddle as if he deserved sole credit for the Greens' first down. He stood upright for a moment behind his center surveying the Blue defense with an air of mastery, then bent over to receive the snap.

As Tim had more or less expected, the play was aimed once again at his end of the line, and he was saddled with the choice of defending against a pass or a run. He was reasonably certain that Luke was determined to prove he could run the ball through Tim's position, and he had a quick hunch that Luke was out to prove it on this play.

It was, in fact, more than a hunch. As the play broke, Tim saw a tip-off on how it would develop. The right half moved a step closer to the center of the line, an indication to Tim that the back wanted an extra step to help him join the blocking more easily. The left half spotted himself a step back from his usual position, suggesting that he, too, would join the other blockers rather than cut across the line as a possible pass receiver.

Tim's brain took in the message without conscious effort, and he planned his defense tactics accordingly. He would either look like a smart guy or a complete chump. Right or wrong, there was no time now to change his mind.

When the play got under way, Tim left his position like a sprinter coming off the blocks. He ignored the surprised end who started upfield as a receiver. Tim angled in toward the Green backfield like a one-man blitz. The Green left half, unprepared for such a move, had to throw his block before he had set himself for the job. His brush block barely slowed Tim's charge. He bore in on Luke, who had not had time to receive the protection of the right half. After a startled look, Luke figured himself for a dead duck if he tried to run, so he did the next best thing. He retreated fast and looked for a downfield receiver.

Luke's left end, whom Tim had ignored, was in fine position to receive a touchdown pass, but Luke was not in fine position to throw one. He had to eat the ball for a big loss or get it away fast. He decided on the latter and threw a wobbly flutter ball that barely cleared the line of scrimmage. A Blue linebacker went into the air and pulled it down for an interception on the Blue thirty-two-yard line.

Luke left the field with angry reluctance. He ignored Tim as a fastidious man ignores some repulsive sight.

Tim also had to leave the field to make way for the Blue offensive team and his stride was not that of a conquering hero. To start with, he did not want to leave the game. More particularly he was nursing doubts as to how his performance would be judged by the exacting coaches. He had stopped the play, sure. He had forced an interception, but the coaches might wonder if he had done it by means of smart football, or if he had taken a wild gamble and managed to come out on the lucky end of the deal. When he reached the bench he got an unexpected break before he had a chance to fret himself into a lather. Monk was just putting down the field phone. He motioned Tim to a spot beside him on the bench.

"I got a call from the tower," said Monk. "Mort Crowder wants to know why you pulled such a fool stunt out there. I'll admit you looked like a real hot shot, but you also left the door wide open for a touchdown, and Mort hates touchdowns when the other team gets them."

Tim felt a cold chill down his back. He was afraid that any attempt to explain his actions would sound like a weak alibi. Wiping damp palms along his pants, he said, "It seemed like a good idea."

"I want a better answer," Monk said harshly.

Tim's faith in his own football instinct began to crumble. He had learned to depend upon it heavily, yet now this same instinct had lured him into a fool stunt. He shrugged and said, "The right half was a step too far to the left if he were going downfield for a pass. The left half was a step too far back. He would have lost that step if he'd intended to go for a pass. I figured they were both set to block."

"Is that all you've got to say?"

"That's all."

"Okay," said Monk. "We just wanted to know if you had a reason for barging in like that. Mort noticed the same thing you did, and so did I."

A feeling of relief rolled over Tim. He said, "I was afraid you. . . ."

"You didn't think we knew our business, huh?" Monk finished for him. "Well, we do." Time out had been called on the field. Monk picked up the phone and pressed the buzzer. "Mort?" he said. "He had it spotted."

Tim knew he might be sticking his neck out with the next question, but he had to ask it anyway. "Did—did I do the right thing on that play?"

Monk shrugged noncommittally. "You stopped the play," he conceded. "Against a smart pro team you might have given up a touchdown. They might have overshifted that way just to fool you."

Monk walked away leaving Tim slightly shaken. His feeling of relief had not lasted very long. He was forced to wonder if his one-man blitz had not been slightly fool-hardy. An experienced cornerback might have been able to achieve the same results without so much risk. Maybe he had made a mistake after all.

The possibility that he had goofed was not pleasant food for thought as he sat on the bench and watched the ball change hands again. Tim started for the field with the defending team, but Monk called him back, sending in another cornerback instead. Tim swallowed a lump of disappointment and went back to the bench. He had not seen much action up to this point and probably he would see no more. Hunching himself on the bench, he sweated out his worries.

He had a lot of time for worrying. The half ended without the Blue team calling upon Tim for further service. Between halves both teams stayed on the field. The coaches reviewed the plays of the first half, criticizing and commending. No one commended Tim, nor, for what it was worth, did he come in for any criticism. He was still an ignored man when the second half got under way.

Tim watched the game with impersonal attention,

but could not remain impersonal about Luke Minty, who was getting a thorough tryout as a quarterback. The Mohawk brass was doing its best to learn if the investment in Luke was a good one or a bad one, and Tim conceded grudgingly that Luke was making it look as if the bonus money had been well spent. It seemed that Tim's chances of becoming a Mohawk quarterback were fading by the minute.

Tim's hopes of getting back into this game were also fading fast. They were going down for the third time when they suddenly came roaring back.

As the teams changed goals for the final period, Monk motioned. "Go in at quarterback for the Blues," he told Tim briefly.

Tim almost blurted out the classic phrase, "Who *me*, Coach?" but managed to restrain himself. He waited briefly for instructions. Monk merely gestured toward the field.

Tim fumbled with the buckle of his helmet as he sprinted toward the teams. He realized that his first big job was to subdue the welter of excitement that was spinning his brain like a whirligig. There was a touch of resentment mixed in too. This late call to run the team was almost like tossing him a bone after the other quarterbacks had been well fed. In the closing minutes of the game he would have little time to show what he could do, particularly if the breaks went against him.

Tim had been tossed into a bad spot, and the knowl-

edge helped quiet his excitement. He would need every bit
of concentration he could summon, and his mind began to
close in on the job at hand before he reached the line of
scrimmage. He was facing a challenge in football tactics,
and, accepting it as that, he began to think in football
terms. It was easier to think about the game than about
injustice or about what the coaches had in store for him.

His first exercise in concentration concerned the men
themselves, both the Blue team and the Green. He had
played with all of them and had catalogued the football
potential of each one. He opened the filing system in his
brain and let the facts come out and fall into their proper
slot. He would have to use what he knew at the right time
and in the right places. He hoped he could.

He checked another important thing as soon as he
reached his team. It was essential to know how the men
would react to him as their new quarterback. Their confidence or lack of it in him would play a large part in the
team's effectiveness. His first impression was encouraging.
The men seemed glad to have him with them. It might
have been because he was another rookie like themselves,
or, better still, they might remember that he handled a
team well in practice and called his signals wisely.

The Blues were not in an enviable position. The team
had made a stubborn goal-line stand and had taken over
the ball on their four-yard line. Two running plays had
brought it to the eleven-yard line, making it third down

with three yards to go for a first down. Tim had to make that yardage if he wanted to stay in the game for more than a single play. If he failed in the first play, he would have to make way for a punter.

The opposing rookies knew enough about pro football to accept the possibility of a pass even this deep in Blue territory. On the other hand, Tim reasoned swiftly, they had to consider that Tim was not a seasoned pro, that he was a fine ball carrier, and that this third down was of tremendous importance to him. The Greens might figure that Tim would not risk a pass under these conditions, and that faith in his own running ability would overbalance faith in his passing arm and in his receivers. Furthermore, he had come into the game cold with no chance to limber up or to get the feel of football action.

With these thoughts zipping through his mind Tim decided on a pass. He had a pair of good receivers in his ends, Bell and Carpenter, but his flanker back, Ken Flagg, possessed a special talent that might be useful at this time. Flagg was a fast deceptive runner with superb balance. He could run a buttonhook pattern with the best of them. He could stop and whirl back toward the line before his defender had a chance to come back with him. Tim called Flagg's signal in the huddle and the flanker nodded approval.

Tim spread his ends and sent Flagg out on the right flank where the defenders might assume he was put to block for a quarterback keeper. Tim put on a good act when the play got under way. He kept the ball and swung to the right, running with the choppy, desperate stride of a man who has but one chance left to make good. He did not pretend to look for pass receivers, and his act went over big. The Green defense moved over fast to cut him down.

Tim plowed to a jarring halt before he reached the side line. A Green linebacker made a try for him and missed. Tim had no time to watch Ken Flagg maneuver. He merely threw the ball toward the middle of the field some ten yards beyond the line of scrimmage, the point where Flagg *should* arrive if he had completed his assignment properly. Flagg got there on the dot and grabbed the ball chest high. He was promptly buried under a pile of Green jerseys, but the play came up with eight yards and a first down for the Blues.

Tim peeled off three more first downs to bring the Blue squad into Green territory. He was concentrating hard on every angle he could figure, on everything he could remember, and on all the small things he was spotting as he went along. He remembered that his left end, Bell, could cut to the right better than to the left and that he was a better receiver from the right side. His other end, Carpenter, was unusually tall, six feet six. His specialty was outjumping his defenders, so Tim kept his passes high to Carpenter.

Tim regretted the limited number of plays available. He felt as if he were driving a car with a balky steering wheel. He noted, too, that some of the plays he used were not as effective as they should have been, and the reason was soon obvious. Most of the men were still playing for themselves, playing for the recognition of the coaches rather than for touchdowns, which represented team effort. The effect of this self-seeking, however, was counterbalanced by the same type of play among the defenders.

Tim mixed his plays well on the ground and in the air. He carried the ball but once, and then in an emergency. He was almost caught behind the line of scrimmage when his receivers were all covered. Twisting free, he swiveled past the line of scrimmage for a six-yard gain.

The defense, beefed up by replacements, got tougher when the Blues moved into Green territory. The attack bogged down on the Green twenty-four-yard line. Tim's third-down pass was batted away, and Tim was replaced by a kicking specialist who came in to try for the field goal. He made it good, which was not much satisfaction to Tim.

As he sat on the bench, his thoughts began to drift away from the technicalities of football. He had a chance to think along personal lines, wondering if his showing as a quarterback had been good enough to satisfy the coaches. He had brought the Blues out of trouble and had carried them into field-goal territory. The fact remained that he had *not* carried them to a touchdown. Had he failed? Were there plays he might have called that would have made the difference between three points and six points? He had no way of knowing. The coaches, of course, would know. The thought was chilling.

When the ball changed hands again, Tim assumed he would be given another chance to run the team—at least *one* more chance. No deal. He watched the remainder of the Rookie Bowl from the bench, full of misery and self-doubt. Nick joined him on the slow walk to the showers.

"Well," said Tim dejectedly, "I guess that's that. I sure can recognize a brush-off when I get one."

"You're jumping to conclusions," Nick accused.

"Could be. I'm running scared, but you've got to admit I didn't see much playing time today."

"Sure, I'll admit it. Don't get the idea that the coaches wait until this game to make their decisions on all the men though. And don't forget that since the day we got in camp we couldn't scratch an ear without some coach writing it down in his book. They may have decided to keep you on the roster before the Rookie Bowl."

"I'm a poor optimist," said Tim.

"So am I. And my case is as shaky as yours. I saw a lot of playing time today, which might mean I was one of the borderline guys."

"That's one way of looking at it," agreed Tim. "But you don't seem to be worried about it."

"Are you nuts?" demanded Nick. "I'm worried sick."

"So that makes two of us."

Chapter Sixteen

There were more than two worried men in the Mohawk camp that night. A flock of rookies and some regulars spent wakeful hours in bed while the coaches sat in conference sifting data, comparing notes, opinions, and convictions. There were painful decisions to be made, responsibilities the coaches did not like but had to shoulder. By the following morning the Mohawk roster would be slashed to forty-five men. The list would be posted at nine o'clock on the locker-room bulletin board.

A lot of good food remained uneaten at breakfast. Tim picked at his scrambled eggs, tried a couple of bites, then gave up. He settled for some coffee and half a slice of toast. There was no need to apologize for his lack of appetite. The others were like him, hollow-eyed and trembling from suspense. Nick was no exception. He and Tim wandered aimlessly about as they waited for the deadline.

All motion was suspended when Monk came from
the office and headed for the training quarters. He walked
with the urgency of a man in a hurry to complete an
unpleasant job. He carried a paper in his hand; it would be
the list of casualties, of course. The men he passed stared
at the paper as if it were a bomb ready to explode. Monk
disappeared into the building. He was soon back to make
an announcement he obviously did not enjoy.

"I've posted a list of the men we can't find places for.
I'm sorry, really sorry, but, well, that's pro football."

Tim expected a stampede into the building, yet there
was nothing of that sort. The movement was slow, reluctant, as if the men were pulling their roots from the
ground. Tim knew how they felt. He wanted desperately
to see that list, but he was almost numb with fear at what
he might find on it. The movement gained speed once the
men had broken contact with the ground. Tim joined the
others, his throat tight, his muscles stiff.

When he was able to get close enough to see the list
he could not read it. The names blurred through no fault
of the typing. Tim's nerves refused to bring his eyes into
clear focus. He corrected the condition with a few blinks
and a hard swallow, and then let his eyes sweep down the
list. He did not see his name or Nick's, but he could not
trust that first swift look, so he steeled himself to take each
name in turn. This time he made sure. Both he and Nick
had survived the cut.

Tim staggered slightly as he moved away. He bumped into Nick, who was also wobbly from shock. They stared at each other wordlessly, managed a pair of feeble grins, then walked across the room and sat down heavily on a bench. Finally they pulled themselves together.

"Whoosh!" Nick broke the silence gustily. "I feel as if I've been run through a cement mixer."

"And I feel as if I've got a collapsed lung. It's hard to breathe."

"You'll make it," Nick encouraged. "We were lucky, pal."

Tim nodded. "Luckier than those poor guys," he said, gesturing toward the stiff-faced men who were plodding from the room.

"I'm sorry for them," agreed Nick. "But maybe some of them will be better off. Now they can settle down and make an honest living. I somehow envy them."

"I don't," Tim said flatly. "Football's my dish and I'll stick with it if I can."

"I think you can."

"Don't be too sure. We made the first big cut, but there are still two more to come."

"I'll worry about that later," said Nick. "Nothing can be as bad as sweating out this first one."

The first congratulations came from Bobo Meeker. He came into the room and walked toward Tim and Nick.

"Nice going," Bobo said. "It'll be fine to have you with us."

"How did you know we made it?" asked Nick. "You didn't go near the list."

Bobo made a vague gesture. "Word gets around," he said.

The proximity of the three lockers had brought Tim, Nick, and Bobo into daily contact that had developed into friendship. They were an oddly assorted trio, but the elements of companionship were there. Although their association had, at first, been limited to the training quarters, it had widened gradually. Both Tim and Nick were surprised and pleased to learn that it had grown more than they believed.

In his slow deliberate manner, Bobo asked, "Have you boys any idea where you're going to live when we get back to New York?"

"We're not even sure we'll get that far," Tim pointed out.

"You'll make it," Bobo said. "It's no great secret anymore. You'll both start the season with the Mohawks."

He let the news sink in. The rookies exchanged wide grins and saved unnecessary words.

Nick said at last, "Thanks, Bobo. And to answer your question, of course we don't have a place to live. We didn't dare push our luck that far."

"No, I guess not," said Bobo reasonably. "Well, I've got an apartment uptown. It's not much, but it's big enough for three. The guys who were sharing it just graduated from Columbia. If you fellows want to help me with the rent, I'd be glad to have you."

"And we'd be glad to come," said Tim promptly.

"Good. And I guess I don't have to warn you that I'll probably be sort of absentminded when I start thinking about building designs and so forth. But maybe you've already found that out."

"Yes, Bobo," Nick assured him. "We've already found that out."

"I drove up here," said Bobo. "You can ride back with me if you want to."

"Sure," accepted Tim with an alacrity that he was later to regret.

The Mohawks broke camp the following day, several weeks earlier than most clubs, a move made necessary by their preseason exhibition schedule. Transportation to these games would be much easier from their home base than from the training camp.

The trip back to New York was an experience in sustained terror for Tim and Nick. Bobo was an excellent driver during the periods when he kept his mind on driving. The other, unpredictable interludes, however, aged his passengers before their time. When Bobo let his mind drift far away into the world of architecture, he drove as if he were intent on suicide.

It was hard to understand how he staved off disaster.

The only explanations Tim's curdled brain could come up with were that Bobo was just lucky or that some deep instinct of self-preservation always came to his rescue in the nick of time. He reached New York with not so much as a dented fender. Relaxed and rested on arrival, he was happily unaware of his near misses on the road and of the motorists' nerves he had shattered.

"I've had it," Tim said weakly, as he staggered onto the pavement.

"That's funny," Bobo said without offense. "A lot of other people have told me the same thing."

"They must have been kidding you," said Nick, his voice unnatural.

Bobo's apartment, as he had warned, was not much, but it was large and comfortable. It consisted of a living room, two bedrooms, a bath, and kitchen. Bobo's bedroom contained an oversized bed to accommodate his huge frame. There were twin beds in the other bedroom. Open bookshelves in the living room were filled with formidable-looking volumes. A large adjustable drawing board was set up near the window.

"A sort of workshop," Bobo apologized. "I've missed it."

"We'll try not to interrupt you when you're busy," Tim said considerately.

Bobo grinned. "You probably couldn't interrupt me without dynamite. When I get my teeth into a construction problem I've got to be jolted out of it."

When the Mohawks settled down to their disciplined routine, Tim and Nick became small cogs in the machine. There were times when Tim became alarmed at the apparent unimportance of his role. He had the frightening feeling that the Mohawks could easily get along without him even though they kept him busy.

The Mohawks played their home games in Titan Stadium, a baseball park that had been the scene of many World Series battles. The Titans were still in residence, involved in a pennant race. The Mohawks, therefore, practiced for the preseason exhibition games at Holden College, on the northern outskirts of the city. Holden, of course, used its stadium for football, so an ample football field outside the stadium was turned over to the Mohawks until they could move into Titan Stadium. The Mohawks' first four games of the regular season were scheduled against teams with available football stadiums. After that the baseball season would be over, and the Mohawks could entertain their opponents at home.

Both Tim and Nick had brief chances to play in the exhibition games and, so far as they could tell, carried out their assignments satisfactorily. Nevertheless, an element of doubt remained. Despite Bobo's calm assurance that everything would be all right, there was a possibility that either man could be among the five players still to be dropped off the roster by the time the season opened. Tim's nerves were not improved by the prospect.

With no other ambition to sustain him, Tim had to

depend on football for whatever future success was in store for him. If the Mohawks released him on waivers, his only hope was a chance for a fresh start with some minor-league team, and inasmuch as no member club of the league was permitted to own a minor-league team, the Mohawks would have no legal claim on him in the event they wanted to recall him as a replacement.

In case of injuries, the replacement rules were strict. A league team could acquire players only by waivers or by trade with other members of the league. There was one exception. If a club was handicapped to the extent of losing four men during the season, it could go outside the league to bring its roster up to thirty-seven. If the loss was greater than four, it could still maintain the club at thirty-seven players. The three-man deficit rule guarded against the shuffling of players who were tabbed as injured.

In a worried moment, Tim asked Nick, "If you get the ax, are you through with football?"

Nick answered without hesitation, "All washed up. I'll figure I've had a fair chance and wasn't good enough to make the grade. I guess that's all I wanted to know to start with. I'll go back to the tool business like a dutiful son with a clear conscience."

"I wish my problem was as simple," Tim said wistfully. "I envy you."

"And you might be surprised to know I envy *you*," said Nick. "No matter what happens, you've got a fight ahead of you. It's big enough to keep you on your toes and keep you scared. There's no chance for you to go to seed or fall into a rut. You'll be living with excitement. As for me, I can only hope for the best when I finally plant myself behind a desk."

The immediate problems of both men were solved a few days later when the vital list was posted. The Mohawks made their final cut to forty active players, and the names of Tim and Nick were on the roster. When Tim's trembling hands and wobbly knees returned to normal, he was a grateful, happy man. He enjoyed the feeling while it lasted, even though he knew that many uncertain moments lay ahead of him. He was now a full-fledged member of the Mohawks. How long he could retain that status depended on many factors.

The first tangible recognition of his new importance came at once. He was issued a play book, the all-important document that contained the club's most guarded secrets, the diagrams and code signals of approximately two hundred plays. It was a loose-leaf notebook of considerable bulk with a tough, flexible cover. Each player possessing a play book was under heavy obligation to protect the book from unauthorized eyes and, to make the obligation more emphatic, a fine of $200 was imposed on any man who could not produce it at the regular check intervals demanded by the club. As a clincher against carelessness, any player who lost or misplaced his book was benched for the following two games unless, of course, the book showed up before that time, and a reasonable explanation was forthcoming.

Tim was certain he had never owned anything as important and desirable as the play book. He handled it with awe, almost as if he had been entrusted with the original copy of the Declaration of Independence. Not only did he thrill with the pride of ownership, but the contents of the book also provided him with fascinating reading. It was more exciting than the most suspense-filled mystery novel he had ever read.

The pages of the book would seem to the average person a jumble of repeated symbols. To Tim each line and cross and circle had its own significance, each one delivered its clear message. In his mind each symbol was a man, each line the assigned course of the football or of a player. Each diagram, in its way, was a mathematical problem, and Tim's natural leaning toward the subject helped him understand them in much less time than most players required.

Added to his mathematical bent was Tim's definite football instinct, a gift that could swiftly translate charts into football action. The diagrams seemed to come alive. He could almost hear the hard contact of the players' bodies. As he turned the pages, he was not surprised to find that the preceding pages were still clearly outlined in his mind. He had that sort of memory. Despite the great number of plays included, most of them were similar in their basic formations. They fell into precise groups. Special individual assignments accounted for the variations within each group.

The book was divided into offensive plays and defensive setups, and Tim was fully aware that he could not concentrate on only one category. He would have preferred studying only the quarterback's offensive plays, but it appeared to Tim that he was being retained as something of a rarity in pro football, a utility man. Most of his action had been divided between quarterback and cornerback. Therefore, he would have to study both offensive and defensive plays, a job he tackled with enthusiasm and found easy.

Chapter Seventeen

The Mohawks got off to a good start. They won their first three road games, lost the fourth, then overwhelmed the formidable Pioneers in the Mohawk opener on their own field. Tim Barlow saw little action in these games, not enough to suit him and not enough to ease his gnawing feeling of uncertainty. He was far from being an established pro, and no one had to write it out for him.

The hours he spent on the bench were not entirely wasted. He learned a lot by watching, but not as much as he would have learned by playing. He studied the tactics of the Mohawks' two fine quarterbacks, Jerry Muller and Buck Fisher, both veterans, both smart and capable. He also had too many opportunities to study the tactics of Luke Minty, who appeared to have been accepted by the Mohawks as the third-string quarterback. Coach Crowder sent Luke into games now and then, when the situation was not too dangerous, to give Muller or Fisher a breathing spell.

Tim tried on those occasions, without too much success, to smother his resentment. The best he could do was to acknowledge that Crowder was sensible to choose an all-American college star over an inexperienced sandlot player. Nevertheless, the choice did not bolster Tim's confidence.

Tim was critical of Luke's play during his brief appearances. He admitted to himself that he was more critical than he should have been. In all fairness, Tim had to concede that not even a college star could run a pro team as it should be run during his first season. Tim was certain he could spot many errors in judgment when Luke was in control, yet perhaps he could not have done any better himself in the heat of a scheduled game. Undoubtedly Crowder was willing to overlook the rough spots in Luke's game in the belief that he would develop into the sort of quarterback he wanted, and Crowder knew that nothing but pro experience could hasten the process.

Tim might have been able to take a more tolerant view of Luke's good fortune had it not been for their contacts off the field. Tim would have been more than willing to avoid the meetings, all of which seemed to be engineered by Luke for no other purpose than to rub Tim's nose in the fact that he was primarily a bench warmer. Luke was snide in a way

that seemed unjustified, even though the two men instinc-
tively disliked each other. He may have felt that Tim was a
longrange threat to his job as third-string quarterback.
Without putting the thought into words, Luke's attitude
suggested that Tim would never reach that goal if he could
do anything to prevent it.

This hostility was merely another worry on a long
list, and Tim began to look for an antidote to the tension.
He found it by sheer accident.

He was alone one evening in the apartment. Bobo
had gone to the library, and Nick was spending the evening with friends from home. When Tim failed to find a
television program that held his interest, he wandered
restlessly around the living room. He stopped in front of
the bookshelves and reached for a book, taking out the
first one his fingers touched, even though he was sure
none of Bobo's weighty volumes could be of interest to
him. *Greek Architecture* was the title of the book.

He opened it at random. The pages parted to a
full-page photograph of the ruins of the Parthenon in
Athens. He was about to close the book when something
stayed his hand. There was no impulse he could define, just
the vague feeling he would lose a thing of lasting beauty
if he put the book back on the shelf. He was reluctant, too,
to remove his eyes from the majestic symmetry of the
shattered building. He turned the page and caught his
breath sharply at another picture of the Parthenon, this

time restored in all its classic glory. He turned slowly, found a chair, sat down, and began to read.

Reading anything but newspapers and fast-moving fiction was a new experience for Tim Barlow. Nonetheless, the visual impact of the Parthenon had stirred a curiosity to learn more about it, and as he read he learned and kept on reading with an eagerness he did not understand.

He learned that the Parthenon had been built in the fifth century under the supervision of Phidias, the Greek considered by many to be the greatest artist of form the world has ever known. The temple was destroyed in 1687 when the Turks, in control of Athens, were being attacked by Venetians attempting to regain the city. The Turks had stored powder in the Parthenon, believing that the statues of the numerous gods would provide protection. The hope was false. A Venetian shell exploded the powder and left the building as it was pictured.

An ambitious undertaking by the city of Nashville, Tennessee, resulted in the reconstruction of the Parthenon, which was opened to the public in 1931. The building was as exact in every detail, except for the construction materials, as patience and exhaustive research could make it. Now it could be seen in its magnificent entirety.

Tim read with amazement that Phidias had solved complicated problems of perspective by creating an optical illusion. No two major lines of the Parthenon are parallel, nor are they exactly equal in length. The columns were built to bulge slightly in the middle, making them appear the same diameter from top to bottom. They were tilted slightly toward the center to make them look straight up and down. They were unevenly spaced with the result that they seemed exactly equally spaced. These overall miracles of architecture permitted the Parthenon to retain perspective when one approached it from a distance.

Tim rested the book on his knees, staring into space as he wondered what was going on inside him. It was as if a tiny thought were taking form and trying hard to find room to grow. In its present form, it merely pointed out to Tim that the Parthenon was man-made, created through the genius of a human mind. Probably no man could duplicate the marvels of the Parthenon, but—and here the thought began to grow—men had conceived and built other structures of beauty, and usefulness, other buildings to house industry and promote gracious living. Furthermore, these achievements would continue as the demand increased.

Tim said aloud, "Why not?" Then impatiently he added, "Don't be a chump." He replaced the book on the shelf and took down another.

Tim continued his experiment for the next few days in secret, almost furtively. It was necessary to convince himself that his new interest was more than a temporary curiosity. Whenever he had a chance to be alone in the apartment, he would select a book at random and read as long as time permitted. Now and then he found himself involved in subjects he did not understand. Discouragement swept over him on these occasions, the depressing knowledge that his slender education had not prepared him to grasp the books he read. Yet instead of warning him to abandon his dream, his inability to cope with what he read unearthed a vein of stubbornness. The books became a challenge.

It was inevitable that Bobo should find out about Tim's secret sessions. He came in unexpectedly one evening and caught him red-handed. Tim made a startled effort to conceal what he was doing, but there was no way to make the heavy volume on Moorish architecture disappear.

"So," accused Bobo. "A bookworm."

Flustered as a kid caught snitching cookies, Tim alibied, "Well, I—I just thought I'd see what made you spend so much money on books."

Bobo seated himself in a chair built to his size. He asked, "Is this your first offense?"

"Well, no, I guess it isn't. I've been sneaking a look at quite a few of those books."

"Like them?" Bobo asked.

Tim studied him closely, searching for amusement in his eyes. There was nothing there but sober interest. He drew a deep breath and admitted, "Yes, I like them. I like them so much that it scares me, Bobo. It almost seems as if I'd started to dig another Panama Canal with nothing but a shovel."

Bobo nodded understandingly. "In other words, you'd like to be an architect."

Tim had not even dared put such a drastic statement into words. The sound of it was so appalling and presumptuous he could not face it. "I—I don't know," he stammered. "It just seems so—so. . . ." his voice trailed off.

Bobo's laughter had a reassuring note as he posed the same question Tim had asked himself. "Why not? It's a long, steep trail, but you can climb it if you want to," he said.

"I want to," Tim said shakily. "Maybe I've flipped my lid. Maybe I'm just plain nuts, but this stuff"—waving toward the shelf of books—"is the most exciting thing that's hit me since I made my first touchdown. I don't know why architecture gets me all stirred up, but it does. For instance, when I was in school, history bored me. I like it now in these books."

"They put a different slant on it," conceded Bobo.

"And that's only a small part of it," said Tim intently. "This business of designing things and watching them take shape is more exciting than anything else. I've been floundering around for years trying to find something beside football to get my teeth into. Maybe this is it."

"Could be," said Bobo. "You're off on the right track at least. How's your math?"

"Okay, I think. It was my best subject in school, and I liked it. I ought to be all right in math."

"You'd better be. You'll need to be good in algebra, trigonometry, and calculus to be sure of your stresses and strains. Architects hate to have their buildings collapse after they've been built! How's your drawing?"

"Drawing?" Tim repeated blankly.

"Sure, drawing, artwork. An architect has to be an artist both with his brains and with his hands. Design, descriptive drawing, painting, photography, and drafting are all a part of his business."

"Whew," breathed Tim. "I guess I hadn't figured quite that far." He then confessed with some embarrassment, "I did use your drawing board a couple of times. I felt like copying a few things I saw in the books."

"Let me see what you did."

Tim went to his room and returned with several sheets of paper. He handed them to Bobo. "They're pretty bad. I didn't take much time," he apologized.

Bobo studied the drawings for a while, then made his comment, "Hmmm."

"As bad as that?" Tim asked sadly.

"Not bad at all," said Bobo. "They're crude, of course, but the lines are strong, confident, and, for the most part, fairly accurate. You seem to have a good eye for perspective and a feeling for design. Those are long steps in the right direction."

"Don't kid me," Tim said seriously.

"I won't," Bobo assured him. "If you want me to, I'll outline a course of work for you."

"Of course I want you to," said Tim. "That is if you really mean it."

"Oh, cut it out," growled Bobo. "And stop being so humble. After all, I'm studying to be a teacher and I might as well use you as a guinea pig. Are you sure you know what you're about to tackle?"

"Not entirely," Tim confessed.

"Five years in college," Bobo said. "After that you'll have to serve three years as an intern. That means three years of humdrum work with an established architecture firm. If you last that long you can hang out your shingle as a practicing architect."

"Wow!" said Tim.

"There'll be a lot of wows before you're through," warned Bobo. "Do you still think you want to have a go at it?"

Tim nodded. "It's not a snap decision. I've had time to think it over. I may fall flat on my face, but it's a chance I want to take."

"You'll need time and money."

"I know. And that's the part that scares me. The only place I can get enough money is from football. I'll have six months off season for the schoolwork, and during the season I can keep on studying, just as you do. If I make the grade as a pro I can afford it, but up to now it's a tossup. If I flunk out as a pro, there's still an outside chance I might have enough guts to keep on plugging to qualify as an architect, but it would take a lot of extra years."

"It would at that," Bobo agreed. "So a lot depends on football."

"Almost *too* much depends on football," Tim said soberly. "Up to now it's been the big thing in my life. It's not anymore. Now football is a means to an end, a springboard to the sort of future I'm sure I want, and that makes football more important than it ever was before."

"You'll make the grade," said Bobo. It was more a statement of encouragement than of assurance.

"Thanks," Tim acknowledged grimly.

Chapter Eighteen

As the season rolled along Tim fought discouragement. He became more and more convinced that the Mohawks had no place for him and probably never would. The club was having a great season. The team worked with smooth, devastating precision. Mort Crowder kept the Mohawks in high gear. They made their own breaks and took advantage of them. As they came roaring down the homestretch, they had a better-than-even chance to be Eastern Division champs. The Broncos, a rough, tough team, were setting off fireworks in the West and were a virtual shoo-in for the Western Division crown. It looked like a head-on clash between the Mohawks and the Broncos for the championship in the play-off game.

For his own consolation Tim told himself that his long periods on the bench were reasonable and not too alarming. He had simply not been needed. The Mohawks had been incredibly lucky. No serious injuries had hit the club, and none of their best players had been put out of action. The club had been able to throw its first teams into every game, and in most of the games they had been needed. Tim certainly could not blame Crowder for using the best line-up available, and there was no reason for the coach to believe that Tim was one of his best players. Luke Minty himself saw very little action and could not expect much as long as Muller and Fisher remained hale and hearty. Tim salvaged what comfort he could from this line of reasoning.

In the meanwhile, Tim studied architecture, pushing himself hard. He was deliberately ruthless for a reason. He had to find out if he could take large doses of the program Bobo mapped out for him. If he bogged down he would have to accept the warning that his first wave of enthusiasm had been a false alarm, and that further study of the subject would be useless.

Nick warned him anxiously, "Don't overdo it. I'm almost as glad as you are that you've found the field you want, and I'd hate to see you ride a good horse to death."

"No chance," Tim assured him. "I've been batting my brains out long enough to know that the deeper I get into the subject the more exciting it is. Bobo seems to think I have the fundamental talent for architecture. I don't think he'd kid me about a thing like that."

"No," said Nick, "he wouldn't. He's not the type. I'm relieved to know you're on the right track."

"I'm on the track, all right, but staying there may be a different matter. As far as the Mohawks are concerned, I'm still riding in the caboose."

"If the club needs you, it'll use you. I'm certain of one thing—with only one scheduled game left, we're both safe until the end of the season. That's bound to mean we'll be called back to training camp."

"Maybe so," said Tim. "It also means we'll be hanging by our fingernails for another year, and I'm not sure I can stand the strain. I wish something *definite* would happen."

Something definite did happen: the roof fell in on Tim. When the play book check day came around Tim couldn't find his. Nick and Bobo joined him in a frantic search of the apartment. A lot of lost objects were brought to light, but the play book was not among them. The deadline for the book-check meeting was an hour away.

Nick finally said, "Let's quit running around like geese and do a little thinking." He turned to Tim. "When did you last have the book?"

Tim tried to put a damper on his panic. Thinking was not easy at the moment. "About two days ago," he said. "I'm sure I had it in the living room." He then admitted honestly, "But I'm not entirely sure. Maybe I'm getting a little like Bobo, sort of absentminded now and then."

Bobo said sadly, "I sometimes forget to lock the door when I go out. Do you suppose somebody could have walked in here and swiped it?"

"Not an ordinary burglar," Nick decided, "because nothing else is missing. If somebody *did* take it, he had a good reason."

An icy shiver ran down Tim's spine. No one had to tell him that the book would be of great value to the Mohawks' opponents, or to somebody who wanted to make contact with the opponents. The fact remained, however, that Tim alone was responsible for the book, and he would have to face the consequences, a $200 fine and a two-game suspension from the club. The fine was unimportant now. A suspension could be disastrous, wiping out all chance for Tim to get into a game for the remainder of the season.

The book could not be found. Tim, pale and shaken, braced himself for an interview with Crowder. He found the coach, as he had hoped, alone in his office at the stadium. After one quick look at Tim's strained face, the coach's own expression showed concern.

"Sit down, Tim," Crowder said. Then when Tim had settled himself stiffly in a chair, the coach guessed, "You've lost the book."

Tim nodded dully.

"Let's hear about it," Crowder said resignedly.

Tim told everything he knew. It wasn't much.

After a thoughtful moment Crowder sighed and said, "It's a serious matter, Tim, but I don't have to tell you that. Books have been lost before. No serious results yet, fortunately. The trouble is, you can never tell. I can't accuse you of anything but carelessness, and I don't intend to. But rules are rules, and you'll have to take the rap. I'm sorry, Tim, but that's the way it is."

"And if I find the book?" Tim asked without much optimism.

"If the book turns up with clear evidence that it's been in safe hands, the suspension will be called off. That's all I can promise. Meanwhile, you can suit up for practice but not for the games."

Tim left the office on lifeless legs. Back in the apartment he continued his fruitless search for the book. During practice session for the next few days the other Mohawks seemed sincerely sympathetic. They knew that the same thing might have happened to any of them.

There was one exception. Luke Minty made no attempt to hide his pleasure with Tim's suspension. He was not foolish enough to gloat publicly; he preferred to needle Tim until he judged the time was ripe to toss the big harpoon.

Finally, in the locker room when many of the Mohawks were on hand, he approached Tim's shoulder and said softly, "Did you get a good price for the play book?"

Luke's timing was exact. He made his move when

Tim's frazzled nerves had reached the breaking point, and Tim reacted just as Luke had undoubtedly hoped he would. Tim whirled and threw a wild roundhouse in Luke's direction. Luke expected it and had time to duck. He accepted it as an invitation to throw a punch at Tim, but Tim was on balance by then and blocked it with his shoulder. Tim's next effort was not wild. A sizzling left hook connected with Luke's jaw, sending him staggering back into the arms of several Mohawks, who had moved in fast to stop the brawl. Luke put on a good show of trying to break away, but the fight was over.

From any angle, though, Tim Barlow was the loser. He was a rookie without a firm position in the club, and no one had to explain to him that starting a fight with one of his teammates could make his position even more precarious. The Mohawks' silence emphasized the point. Tim's anger drained away as he turned back to his locker. There was just emptiness inside him.

He obeyed another summons to Mort Crowder's office the following morning. Tim braced himself for the chewing out he expected from the coach, but it turned out to be much worse than that. Crowder had the look of a man facing an unpleasant job. He tackled it head on. "Do you know a character by the name of Jake Minski?"

Tim thought for a moment, then asked, "Isn't he the funny little guy who hangs around outside the stadium almost every day? I've seen him, but I don't know him."

"Do you know what he does for a living?"

"I've heard he's some sort of a gambler."

"He's a bookie," said Crowder with distaste, "a little two-bit bookie. He tries to act important by striking up conversations with the players and pretending he knows them. We've always considered him good for a laugh."

Tim waited warily. He didn't like the way things were shaping up. Crowder plunged ahead. "Luke Minty told me he saw you hand Minski a folded newspaper the other day. Is that true?"

"Why, yes," said Tim. "He asked me if I was through with the paper. I said I was and handed it to him."

"Was anything inside that paper?"

Tim's jaw dropped. His first reaction was one of quick alarm, his next of savage anger. His mouth snapped shut; his eyes shot sparks that crackled. He was half out of his chair before he managed to control his temper. Slowly he sank back.

"The play book was not inside that paper," he said stiffly.

"That's all I need to know," said Crowder gruffly. "I had to ask those questions, Tim. It's my job. It's a nasty matter, a nasty accusation, and I had to clear it up."

"Sure," conceded Tim. He was thinking clearly now as he went on, "So let's clear it up all the way. If I sold the book, would I be stupid enough to sell it to a little guy like Minski? He couldn't pay me a fraction of what it would be worth to someone else."

"I'd considered that," said Crowder.

"And would I be fool enough to get rid of the book itself rather than make a copy of the plays? Better than that, I could sit down with somebody and chart every play in the book from memory."

"You *what?*" demanded Crowder.

"I've got a funny brain," said Tim. "Signals and diagrams stick with me."

"Well, I'll be," said Crowder, obviously impressed and obviously glad to steer the interview to a more pleasant subject. "That's quite a gift, Tim, particularly for a quarterback. The trick is to use the right play at the right time, and not to call a tricky or obscure play the men might be a little fuzzy on."

"Yes," said Tim noncommittally.

With the air of a man who has pulled himself out of a bad hole, the coach said, "Well now, I'm sorry that this unpleasant business had to come up, but as far as I'm concerned you're in the clear. I know that you and Minty aren't exactly buddies, but don't throw any more punches in the locker room. It's bad for team morale."

Club morale was nothing to be tampered with during the few days before the final scheduled game against the Hawks. A win could clinch the Eastern title for the Mohawks. Coach Crowder brought the men to a fine edge of irritable fitness, which paid off in a final score of 27–17. The Mohawks celebrated in a mild way, restricted by the knowledge that the rampaging Broncos had also won their sectional title and were eager to tear the Mohawks into little pieces in the playoff game two weeks away. The game would be played on the Mohawks' home field, a great break for Mohawk fans lucky enough to get tickets.

With the skill of long experience, Coach Crowder kept his men on edge. Tim Barlow could not share their excitement. He would not be eligible for the play-off game, even though he might be needed. His suspension would still be in effect. He was allowed to join the final light practice sessions, but they held no interest for him, and he went through the motions automatically.

When the big day finally arrived, it held small significance for Tim except from a financial angle. He could not be indifferent to the seventy percent of the net receipts of the world championship game that would go to the players on the first three teams of each conference. Seventy-five thousand dollars would be taken off the top for the players on the third-place teams and one hundred thousand for the players on the second-place teams. Whatever was left, and it would be plenty, would be divided sixty percent to the winners and forty percent to the losers of the championship game. Tim was by no means sure of getting a full share as either a winner or a loser. His value to the team had been so doubtful that his share would be determined by a vote of the regular members. He would be glad to get the extra cash, of course, but the money would be small consolation for his misery and uncertainty of the past season.

Nick and Bobo, both on edge, prowled restlessly around the apartment, trying to kill time before the briefing session at the stadium. Tim worked listlessly on a crossword puzzle, finding it hard to come up with even the simplest words. The phone rang. Bobo answered it.

"Yes, he's here," said Bobo. "I'll call him." He turned from the phone. "It's for you, Tim."

Tim wondered without too much interest who would call him at this time. He picked up the receiver and said, "Hello."

A woman's voice at the other end inquired, "Is this Mr. Tim Barlow?"

"Yes, it is," acknowledged Tim.

"My name is Mrs. Blanding. I'm in the circulation department of the public library. One of my assistants was checking the volumes in our architecture section when she came across a strange book with your name, address, and telephone number in it."

"Yes?" said Tim, completely puzzled.

"It's a large loose-leaf notebook filled with mysterious diagrams, which I assume are football plays. Do you recognize the book by that description?"

Tim's voice jammed in his throat. He finally managed a weak croak, "Yes, it's mine." The words unlocked his throat and more words came tumbling out, his voice shrill and verging on hysteria. "It's mine! It's my play book! I thought it was lost! I've been looking for it and . . ."

"Now take it easy, young man," said the calm,

amused voice at the other end. "Everything is under control. The book will be waiting for you in my office whenever you want to pick it up."

"I'll be there right away!" yelled Tim. He hauled in a deep breath and turned down his volume. "Thanks, Mrs. Blanding. Thank you very, very much."

"Not at all. I'm glad we found it. I'll expect you."

In a happy daze Tim returned the phone to its cradle. Gathering the good news from Tim's side of the conversation, Nick let out a whoop. Bobo stood frozen in the middle of the floor. His face had a stricken look.

"I did it," he said hoarsely. "It was my fault all along."

The picture was clear enough now, yet Tim, in his moment of great happiness, could hold no resentment against his absentminded friend. "Forget it," Tim told Bobo. "We've got the book and that's all that matters."

"It was my fault," insisted Bobo on the verge of tears. "I must have gathered it up with some other stuff I was taking back to the library. I spend so much time there that I'm sort of a privileged character, and Mrs. Blanding gives me a free run of the architecture division. In my half-witted way I must have put your book back on the shelf with the other books. I'm sorry, Tim. Maybe some day I can square myself."

"Forget it," Tim repeated. "We've got the book. I'm on my way right now to pick it up."

Chapter Nineteen

After Tim retrieved his precious play book he went directly to the stadium for the pregame briefing, a meeting he looked forward to more than he had believed possible an hour ago. He was certain that, under the conditions, the suspension would be lifted. He could, therefore, listen to the briefing with some degree of interest, even though the chances were remote that he would have a chance to use the information Crowder would cram into the men. At least Tim could now attend as an active player rather than as an outsider.

Crowder lost no time in telling Tim, "I've been in touch with Bobo. He was ready to cut his throat, but I talked him out of it. He explained everything and, of course, you're on the squad again. I revoked your fine and slapped it on Bobo. He seemed to cheer up a little."

The briefing session followed the familiar pattern, but each Mohawk, knowing the vital importance of this game, sat tautly in his chair and stretched his brain to its full capacity. After a husky lunch served at the stadium by a caterer, they were told to get what rest they could and to think about the things the coach had told them in the briefing.

The Mohawks were permitted to use the executives' lounge at the rear of the mezzanine section of the stadium. Tim and Nick found adjoining chairs in a corner. Each man was wrapped up in his own thoughts.

Nick broke the silence. "This is the big one."

"Yes," said Tim. Then suddenly he turned his eyes toward Nick as he sensed something in Nick's tone. The remark had been more than a casual statement.

"You've got a funny look. What gives?" demanded Tim.

"It'll be my last game, Tim. I'm leaving football, and I'd like to check out with a good performance."

It took Tim several moments to adjust his thoughts as he fought against a sense of shock and loss. He finally said, "I should have guessed it. You've been acting strange the last few days."

Nick nodded. "I suppose I have. The decision wasn't easy, but I had to make it. I've convinced myself I can play pro football and that's what I set out to do. It'll be a whole lot easier now to go back where I belong. The longer I wait the harder it will be. If I wait until I'm burned out or permanently injured as a football player, I won't deserve much credit for going back to the tool business. If I go back now I can look myself straight in the face, and I'm sure that sooner or later I'll be a help to Dad. Does that make sense?"

"Yes," conceded Tim reluctantly, "it makes a lot of sense."

An hour before game time Tim climbed into his uniform eagerly. He realized his emotion was probably a little pitiful in view of the negligible chance he had of getting a spot of gridiron dirt on the uniform. It was comforting to wear it just the same. He even enjoyed a small feeling of importance when he joined the squad for its pregame warm-up.

The day was fine, the weather cool and brisk. With a dry, fast field, the conditions favored the Mohawks, who would have to depend on their speed and maneuverability to match the grinding power of the Broncos. The game would be a battle between teams of different styles, the boxer versus the mauler.

When the game was finally called, the stadium was rocking to the clamor of 65,000 fans, some of whom had been happy, even lucky, to get seats in the temporary bleachers behind the goal line. Most of the fans were, of course, for the Mohawks. They had worked themselves into a splendid state of hatred against a team that had built itself a reputation as the bogey man of football, a fearsome squad of bruisers.

The Broncos' reputation, however formidable, had small effect upon the Mohawks, who were ready for the big one. They charged onto the field, after winning the toss and electing to receive, like a pack of unleashed hounds. The suicide squad pulled in the kickoff on the goal line and ran it back to their own thirty-six-yard line, a fine start that pleased the fans. The two teams changed platoons, and the game got under way in earnest.

Jerry Muller, as expected, got the starting assignment as quarterback. If there were any early jitters among the Mohawks, Jerry Muller, with his superb confidence and unhurried manner, was the man to cure them. Strolling calmly from the huddle, he regarded the glowering Broncos with a calm amusement that reduced their head of steam by several pounds. Before they were able to regain the pressure, Jerry flipped a side-line pass to his great receiving end, Clint Stack. The play was good for sixteen yards and placed the ball two yards inside Bronco territory.

Jerry went on from there to jab the Broncos dizzy. A feint here, a thrust there, a light tap to divert attention, then a solid punch where it hurt the most. He had a fresh team, an alert and eager team, and he made the most of it. He kept the Broncos scrambling for balance, a balance they did not attain in time. A twelve-yard pass was hauled in by Clint Stack in the coffin corner. The extra-point kick split the center of the goalposts, and the Mohawks jumped into an early 7–0 lead.

The Mohawks and their fans were very pleased. The Broncos were not pleased at all. Their offensive team came charging onto the field with a determination that shook the ground. The Mohawk defenders, quite unawed, met them head-on with a swift-charging defense that equalized the difference in weight between the two lines. The Broncos kept their bulldozer in high gear for three first downs and brought the ball into Mohawk territory on the thirty-eight-yard line. The Mohawks dug in to hold a pair of line plays to six yards. An incomplete pass left the Broncos in a fourth-and-four situation. Their field-goal specialist came in. He uncorked a fine kick, which brought the Broncos into the scoring column, 7–3.

The Mohawks went on the attack again, retaining enough of their early drive to throw a scare into the Broncos. They moved the ball past midfield. Jerry heaved a long one. He connected with his fleet halfback, Stu Klein. Stu romped into the end zone. The Mohawk fans exploded with joy, then collapsed in misery when an offside penalty was called against their boys. The ball came back and the touchdown was wiped out.

The bitter disappointment robbed the Mohawks of a little zing. Jerry tried, but could not get them rolling at full speed until they had recovered from the jolt. Meanwhile, the Broncos continued to work on Jerry. Tim saw what was going on and was not surprised. The Broncos' reputation was well known and accepted. They advertised themselves as a team playing rough, hard-nosed football, strictly within the rules, an evaluation no one but the Broncos accepted literally.

The roughness of the game was evident enough. The strictly-within-the-rules part was subject to a lot of raised eyebrows, because any clever football hoodlum can get in a lot of dirty stuff under the cover of a pile of human bodies. The pros' unwritten code warned against complaints, particularly if the offenses could not be proved, and seldom could they be proved against the Broncos.

Facts could not be ignored, however, and the case against the Broncos was strengthened by the long list of injuries suffered by opposing teams throughout the season. Their tactics were unmistakable and simple. If an opposing player posed too great a threat, the word went out to put the poor guy out of action, and it was clear that Jerry Muller posed too great a threat.

The Broncos, though, were tangling with a tough old rooster, who had been through the wars for many years. Muller had learned every trick of self-protection known and had invented some himself. He had long since learned the most important one—don't flinch. Take everything they can dish out and don't retreat an inch. Any pro quarterback who deserves the title knows that eleven pairs of eyes on the field, and a lot more on the bench, are watching for that instant of hesitation, for that fleeting look of apprehension that will say a beat-up quarterback has had almost enough. It means his timing has been ruined, that his passes will lack accuracy.

The Broncos kept the pressure on Jerry for the remainder of the period. They blitzed him, hit him high and low, and roughed him in the pileups with no sign that they were making an impression. Jerry Muller had all the guts he needed. He retaliated with another touchdown pass plus the conversion. The Broncos kicked another field goal. At the end of the period the score was 14–6.

Despite Jerry's assurance that he was okay, Coach Crowder kept him on the bench for a rest when the second quarter got under way. Buck Fisher took over. He did a fine job in his flashy style, but the Bronco defense had got its teeth into the game and hung on stubbornly. The Bronco offensive unit also came in for its share of glory, even though it needed a good break to put the score across. The Mohawks lost the ball on a fumble deep in their own territory. Turning on their full ground power, the Broncos rammed across the goal line for their first touchdown. They kicked the extra point, making the score 14–13.

When Buck Fisher had absorbed his share of Bronco bruising toward the end of the second period, Jerry Muller was sent in again. The Broncos took up where they had left off on him. They continued their program of attrition and cheerfully accepted a couple of stiff penalties when their tactics misfired and a couple of their goons got caught red-handed. The penalties hurt, but did not side-track the Broncos from their main goal. In the late minutes of the period Jerry was snowed under by a blitz. When he got out from under the pile, he had a badly twisted ankle. The Broncos watched with blank faces as a pair of Jerry's teammates helped him from the field. The defensive team had done the job assigned to it. The individual Bronco responsible for the injury was helped from the field after the next play with a dislocated knee. The swap was a poor one. The guilty Bronco was expendable whereas Jerry Muller was not. His loss to the Mohawks was a crippling blow.

The half ended with the Mohawks still clinging to their one-point lead. The Broncos received the kickoff at the start of the second half and put their steamroller into action. It was grinding out yardage like a juggernaut until, deep in Mohawk territory, a defensive end crashed through on the third down to drop the ball carrier for a three-yard loss on the twenty-nine-yard line. The Broncos tried another field goal on the fourth down and made it good. They went into the lead for the first time in the game, 16–14.

Buck Fisher, now the number-one quarterback, took over for the Mohawks after the kickoff had been run back to the twenty-four-yard line. His flashy style was always a threat to any defensive team. With Jerry permanently out of the game, though, the Broncos were free to set themselves for Buck's tactics alone. Things then became a little easier for them.

In the meanwhile, they did not neglect their campaign to put pressure on the quarterback. They gave Buck a rough time despite the efforts of the Mohawk line to protect him on the pass plays. Then, to make their position even more secure, they zeroed in on the Mohawks' star receiver, Clint Stack. A linebacker caught Stack at the vulnerable moment when he was reaching high into the air to snag a pass. The Bronco threw a wicked tackle while Stack was still off the ground, but after he had caught the ball. It was all fair and legal, a small consolation to Clint Stack, who was taken from the game with a cracked rib.

Nick Jeffer was sent in to replace Stack. The selection was a great compliment to a rookie, and Tim was delighted to see Nick get a chance, even though he knew that Nick's presence in the game would be very brief if he failed in the job assigned to him. Nick did not fail. He made a pair of brilliant side-line catches before the Broncos accepted him as a serious threat. Nick's catches were important. They gave the Mohawks a first down on the twenty-one-yard line. Three downs netted but six yards, and the Mohawks went for the field goal. The kick was good, and the Mohawks took the lead again, 17–16.

On the surface the game was shaping into a seesaw battle. Beneath the surface it was something else again. The Bronco defense was well aware of its remaining task—nail the quarterback. They went about it doggedly. Buck took a severe mauling, but stood up to it. Ironically, when Buck's injury came, it could not be blamed entirely on the Broncos. He got a pass away, but on the follow-through his hand hit the helmet of a charging Bronco. Buck broke a finger. The accident was a freak; nevertheless, Buck Fisher had also completed his football season.

With his two regular quarterbacks out of business Coach Crowder gave the nod to Luke Minty. Tim tried to smother his resentment with the knowledge that the coach's choice was logical. He also had to give Luke credit for the eagerness with which he left the bench to charge into the hungry jaws of the waiting Broncos. Luke was obviously full of confidence and grateful for the chance in spite of the knowledge that the Broncos were prepared to treat him as they had treated Buck and Jerry.

Tim even hoped that Luke would do the job and do it well. His feeling had nothing to do with Luke's welfare; his concern was entirely for the Mohawks. Tim had not realized before how closely he identified with the club despite his minor role. It seemed terribly important now that the Mohawks should win, and if Luke could do the job, so much the better.

It looked, at first, as if Luke might turn the trick. He

entered the game on second down and six with the ball on the Mohawk forty-one-yard line. Luke swung wide for a pass, found his receivers covered, and took off for a fine twelve-yard run. Thus encouraged, he tried another keeper, a bad mistake against a smart, rough defensive team. He was racked up for a four-yard loss.

The next two downs did not repair the damage, and the Mohawk were forced to kick. The runback went all the way. Every Bronco happened to be in the right place and every Mohawk in the wrong place. It was a heartbreaker. The extra point brought the score to 23–17 with the Mohawks on the short end. The Mohawk fans were squirming in distress.

What happened after that was clear to Tim, and he could not blame Luke entirely. The team itself was more or less at fault. The men were accustomed to the leadership of either Jerry or Buck and could not accept Luke as a comparable replacement. They tried, but their desperate efforts only made things worse by destroying the fine timing so essential to attack.

Their lack of confidence may have had its effect on Luke, yet Tim could not be entirely sure. He could see, however, that Luke was showing definite flaws in leadership, and undoubtedly Coach Crowder was unhappily observing the same flaws. The Mohawk defense was doing a heroic job containing the power of the Bronco offense, but when the Mohawk offensive unit went into action behind Luke Minty, it offered little hope of overcoming the Bronco lead.

Luke appeared to be standing up fairly well under the relentless battering of the Bronco defenders. His chief weakness, as nearly as Tim could analyze it, was a lack of promptness in calling audibles. When the Broncos came up with a surprise defense formation that could threaten the signal called in the huddle, it was Luke's job to use an audible and change that signal promptly to one that was suitable for the new defense, one that would exploit its weakness.

Luke was not calling audibles efficiently. Too often he let the huddle signal stand with the result that the Mohawks banged into a defense designed to stop that very play. The situation was most unhelpful to an attacking team's morale, because the men themselves were bound to realize what was going on. Luke could probably be excused because of limited experience, but excusing him did the Mohawks no good at all.

On the other hand, Luke's uncertainty helped the Broncos a lot. They blitzed him without mercy. There were measures to counter the blitz, but Luke seemed too confused to adopt them. He began to get up from the ground more slowly than at first, and when, for the first time, he retreated just that fraction of a step that indicated he'd had almost enough, the Broncos knew they'd done their job again. They had a frightened quarterback to work

on now, and a frightened quarterback does not last long
against a team of pros. Tim almost felt sorry for Luke.
Then he began to feel sorry for himself.

Coach Crowder, pacing the side line like a restless
bear, turned toward the bench. His face, bleak and gray
beneath his tan, was the face of a man backed against the
wall and fighting for his life. He stopped in front of Tim.
"Okay, Tim, get your arm warmed up. You'll be replacing
Minty."

Tim froze for an instant in his place. He couldn't
speak, so he merely nodded and forced his legs to lift him
off the bench. At the coach's nod, another man got up to
help Tim with his warm-up. They began to toss a football
back and forth.

Tim's moves were automatic at first. He was angry at
himself for being caught completely unprepared. He told
himself that any half-wit could have read the signs. He
should have known by watching that the Mohawks' quarterback reserve had dwindled to the point where the coach
would have to scrape the bottom of the barrel. There was
no one left now but Tim Barlow, a rookie with a sandlot
background. Small wonder Crowder looked like a man
with a pistol pointed at his head.

The coach's genuine despair was no compliment to
Tim, yet Crowder's attitude of hopeless resignation turned
out to be the goad that jarred Tim out of his first shock.
He did not like to be regarded as a weak, inadequate

replacement. Tim's indignation was a healthy boost to his morale, which needed boosting at the moment.

As he passed the football back and forth he realized he was deliberately avoiding the main issue, the real significance of the thing he had been called upon to do. Apprehensively he faced the thought of what this chance to quarterback the Mohawks in their desperate moment might mean to him.

Too much depended on it. It was hardly fair to put him on this spot. His future was at stake, a fact he had to look straight in the eye. Should he handle the team well, or even fairly well, he might establish himself with the Mohawks, which meant that he would have a chance to finish the education he now so desperately wanted. Should he fail (his stomach shriveled at the thought) he had no plans beyond the end of the game.

He was afraid that once in the game he could not keep this anxiety from his mind. If he dwelt upon the possibility of failure rather than upon the game of football, he was sunk for sure. There was no way to be certain in advance how his brain might function when the chips were down. He could only wait.

The wait was longer than he cared for. When the Broncos batted down one of Minty's passes, the Mohawks were forced to kick on fourth down. Making way for the kicking specialist, Luke came off the field with a dismal air. Whatever other failings Luke might have, he wasn't stupid.

He knew he had wilted under big-league pressure, and he knew that the fact was evident to everyone. To put a clincher on the matter, he had seen Tim Barlow warming up along the side line.

The Broncos ground out another touchdown. They hammered their way into the end zone against a stubborn team that had lost a vital spark. The Mohawk defense, though savage, had an aimless quality. The men fought hard, but the very violence of their effort hampered their coordination. They were battling as much against discouragement as they were against the Broncos. The Broncos missed the try for the extra point, but they were not bothered. With the score 29–17, they were in the driver's seat and knew it.

Chapter Twenty

When the suicide squad went out to receive the kickoff, Tim finished his warm-up and moved close to Crowder for instructions. The coach merely gestured toward the field and kept silent, leaving Tim the choice of several guesses as to what the silence meant.

Crowder might not want to fill a rookie's mind with tactics and instructions while he was still fighting against nerves. Perhaps he trusted Tim's football instinct and judgment. Tim discarded that flattering possibility. He settled on the logical assumption that the coach would wait until the action started before sending in instructions by replacements.

Meanwhile, Tim had a rugged problem of his own. So much, everything in fact, depended on his mental attitude when he went into the game. Yet, as he waited for the kickoff, his thoughts bounced around uncontrollably. He could only hope that the feel of the gridiron beneath his cleats would settle him down.

The Mohawks did a mediocre job of running back the kickoff to the twenty-four-yard line. The offensive team came off the bench from where they had been watching Tim with speculative eyes. Coach Crowder shoved Tim gently toward the field. The pressure of the coach's fingers on his arm gave Tim the wordless message of good luck.

Tim started onto the field, fearfully testing the theory that had never failed him in the past, the belief that something magic flowed into his body when his cleats met turf. The miracle unfolded promptly. Tim stepped into another world, a world hemmed in by the four sides of a football field. He was a football player now, and football ruled his thoughts.

He grunted with relief, then opened his mind to absorb impressions from the turbulence about him. It struck him first that the Mohawks were impassive, virtually resigned to take a beating. With the exception of Nick and Bobo, who seemed delighted to have Tim in the game, the attitude of the other Mohawks toward Tim was non-committal, quite as if they had told themselves, "So what? He can't be any worse than Luke."

Nevertheless, the Mohawks, prepared for the worst, watched Tim closely as they moved into the huddle. They were searching for some sign of rookie nerves. There were puzzled looks on some Mohawk faces when Tim showed merely an intent, tight concentration. The Mohawks seemed unable to explain his attitude to themselves. It put them in company with Tim, who could not explain it to himself. He called the signal in a crisp, authoritative voice. A hopeful quiver ran down several Mohawk spines.

When the Mohawks came to the line of scrimmage, Tim stood erect for a moment letting his eyes sweep across the Broncos. He saw what he had been prepared to see, a team of smug, thoroughly assured football players, who had pulled the teeth from the Mohawk attack by handily disposing of three quarterbacks. They now stared hungrily at Tim. Their eyes seemed to ask, "How long do you expect to stay in there, sonny? There's nothing we like better than a fourth-string rookie quarterback. We're going to get you, and fast."

Tim had called his first signal in anticipation of this sort of welcome. He figured that even at the risk of giving up some yardage, the Broncos would waste no time in their campaign to go after another Mohawk quarterback. Tim split his ends and sent out his flanker, Stu Klein, in a pass-play formation. When the ball came back from the big center, Tom Duff, Tim retreated a few steps, cocked his arm, and watched the Bronco blitz come storming at him.

Before it hit, Tim's arm swept down for a short hand-off to his fullback, Joe Culler, who slammed into the left side of the line through a hole left by the eager blitzers.

He peeled off six yards before one of the remaining line-backers pulled him down. Tim came out from under the pile of Broncos not much the worse for wear. He had been lucky on that first play, lucky that he had guessed right and lucky that it had gone for a gain. Its success made a slight difference in the Mohawk huddle. The men were not yet ready to accept Tim as the solution to their problem, but their hopes were rising.

Tim called another line play, taking the chance he might get the same reaction from the Broncos. The instant he reached the line, however, he knew he had guessed wrong. Not wanting to be caught twice in the same blunder, the Broncos had modified their defense so that the linebackers were fairly tight, but not as tight as they would have been for a blitz.

Tim got another swift impression from the Broncos. His intuition made him almost certain they were expecting another running play. They probably reasoned that a rookie quarterback, successful on the first play, would be tempted to give it another try. They may have reasoned, too, that a man fresh off the bench, and an inexperienced man at that, would be reluctant to limber up his passing arm so deep in his own territory. Tim played his hunch.

He called an audible, being careful, without conscious decision, to call one that would not cause a shift in the present formation and give the Broncos a chance to change their defense. Tim had a good voice for audibles, clear and penetrating. He gave the change of signals a moment to sink in, then took the snap from Duff.

He faded a few steps, cocked his arm, and braced himself. It was a look-in pass, a tricky play to attempt, also a tricky one to defend against. Tim kept his vision wide to watch for slipups requiring a change of tactics. Everything looked fine. Nick, after a fake downfield, angled sharply through the Bronco backfield. Tim's job was to catch him on the wing, to whip the pass through with enough lead to catch Nick on the run.

Tim pulled it off, and so did Nick. Nick grabbed the ball shoulder high without breaking stride. He was finally forced out of bounds, but not until he had whacked off fourteen yards. Tim's knees were a little weak, a condition that did not last long. He had chosen a severe task for himself on his first pass, a pinpoint operation with a wide margin for failure. It had clicked, however, and that's all Tim had to know. His arm and his eye were ready for more action.

The atmosphere in the huddle improved another notch. Tim could feel it. The men were looking at him in a puzzled way, as if trying to assure themselves that they could believe what they were seeing. Most of them had played with Tim before in brief scrimmages, but none of them had played with him at a time like this, when the pressure was almost unbearable and when so much depended on the outcome of a game. They had every right to expect caution and uncertainty from an inexperienced rookie like Tim Barlow, yet none of these things were evident as yet. Tim's poise was thoroughly reassuring.

It may have been the successful audible that gave the Mohawks food for pleasant thought. As many as two-thirds of the signals called in a pro game are audibles. It is an absolute necessity that a quarterback be able to call them well. The original signal must be called in the huddle. If the defense changes at the line of scrimmage in a way to threaten the play, the signal must be changed.

The Mohawks used a letter code to make the change. At the start of each signal in the huddle the quarterback called out some letter of the alphabet. It was the "live" letter, which each man had to remember. If the signals needed changing at the line, the quarterback called out the live letter, meaning that an entirely new signal would follow. If he called some other letter than the live one, the huddle signal stood. Inasmuch as he always chattered off a signal before the play broke, the defense had no way of knowing whether the signal they heard was genuine.

The audible system depends entirely on the quarterback for success or failure. He has but a few seconds to size up any surprise defense and to select a play to take advantage of whatever weakness he spots in the new defense. He cannot use guesswork. Success requires a swift mind and a lot of football instinct immune to pressure. Luke Minty had failed the Mohawks in his calling of audibles, and they were clearly hoping that Tim's first success was not a bit of luck.

The completion of the tricky look-in pass gave the Broncos something to think about. They had not been briefed on this upstart kid fresh from the sandlots, and it was hard for them to accept the fact that he might be dangerous. They would be fools, however, to take too much for granted. Therefore, they kept a cautious eye on Tim until they learned more about him.

The uncertainty of the Broncos was the slim advantage Tim held for the moment. He was smart enough to know it would not last very long. The Broncos knew that Tim could throw a short, accurate pass. Throwing the bomb was another matter, and the Broncos could only guess about that. Tim decided to let them guess as long as he could move the team without heaving the long one.

With the ball on the Mohawk forty-four-yard line, Tim decided to risk another pass, knowing full well the probable consequences of success. Once convinced that Tim was a passing quarterback the Broncos would try to eliminate him as they had eliminated Jerry Muller and Buck Fisher. It was an occupational hazard Tim had to accept, and he was glad to find he could face it without too much concern. He was enjoying life, reveling in the tremendous thrill of playing football, playing for keeps.

The Mohawks came to the line with a snap that had been absent in the third period until now. Tim barked his audible. It did not change the huddle signal, and when the Mohawks came out with their flanker and spread ends, the Broncos paid Tim the compliment of loosening their defense to cover the possible receiver. Tim took a few fancy steps, ducked under the flailing arm of a big lineman, then flipped the ball to his safety valve, the other halfback, Ken Tinker, who coasted unattended in the Mohawk backfield. The pass was swift and accurate, beating the lunge of a defensive back who tried to knock it down. Tinker cut back through a hole and wiggled through the Bronco backfield for eight yards to the Bronco forty-eight-yard line.

In the huddle the Mohawks were quivering with impatience, willing to accept the unexpected gift that Tim was handing them. Tim called the most obvious signal in the world, a line plunge, to pick up two yards and a first down. He did it for a purpose. He had to know if the men were as keyed up as they appeared to be. He was giving them a chance to prove it by asking them to blast the formidable Bronco line.

Tim covered himself in one respect, however. Quick instinct and the look in Bobo Meeker's eyes told Tim that Bobo was all primed for the attack. He called the play through Bobo's guard position, and Tim's hunch was sound. Bobo's huge bulk moved with the speed of a lightweight sprinter off his marks. The Broncos were not fooled. They were waiting for the play and little good it did them. They might as well have tried to stop an angry rhinoceros. Bobo's mighty grunt could be heard above the clash of bodies. He ripped a wide hole in the Bronco line, kept on going, and took out a Bronco linebacker. Joe Culler hit the hole on Bobo's heels. He went in low and hard. Before they brought him down he had ground out six more yards, giving the Broncos a good sample of their own powerhouse technique.

The Broncos called time out to talk things over. They had to concede that the new quarterback was dangerous. If he was merely lucky he might continue to be lucky. They dared not underestimate him. The kid could pass, he could handle the ball smoothly behind the line, and he could think. The boy must go—and soon.

The Broncos' first move toward this end could hardly be mistaken. A replacement came galloping onto the field, a massive man with blue jowls and a low forehead. He was a headhunter, a man who does not last long in a pro-football game and is not expected to. His sidelong looks in Tim's direction confirmed his intentions. Tim Barlow was the target for today.

The man would have his chance because the Broncos would provide one for him. There was nothing Tim could do except try to keep Blue Jowl from hitting him on the blind side. With a screen pass set up for the next play, Tim let the huddle signal stand when the Broncos grouped themselves for the inevitable blitz.

It came with the snap of the ball. Tim got away a

short pass, then whirled to meet the Bronco hatchet man. He was not there. Bobo had dropped back to block for the screen, but he had accomplished more than blocking. Tim saw only the end result of Bobo's move. Blue Jowl was sprawled on the ground cold as an ice cube. Bobo was already on his feet regarding his handiwork with interest. The referee came within a hair of dropping his foul signal on the ground before deciding Bobo's action had been legal.

Bobo explained to Tim, "He was a bad boy. Stupid, too. He had his eye on you instead of me. Most regrettable—for him. I don't think we'll be bothered by any more trigger men."

"Thanks, Bobo," Tim said quietly.

"Tut, tut." Bobo brushed him off. "I owe you plenty, kid."

The screen play paid off well. Thanks to the Bronco concentration on the blitz, Stu Klein had scooted down the side line for twelve yards before the safety man came up to bounce him out. The Mohawks had a first down on the Bronco thirty-yard line.

There the Broncos pulled in their defense and made things tough. A brilliant defense play slapped a touchdown pass from Nick Jeffer's fingertips. The period ended at that point, leaving the Mohawks still thirty yards from the end zone with ten yards to go for a first down. While the teams changed goals Tim walked with his head down, thinking hard, trying to get an inspiration. He drew a blank.

When play got under way, Tim sent Stu Klein on an end sweep after faking a short pass across the line. The call looked good until Stu, cutting sharply back toward the line, caught a soft spot in the turf. It wouldn't hold his cleats. Stu skidded and went down, making only a two-yard gain.

Third down, eight to go, a rough situation for a rookie quarterback. Tim expected a signal or advice of some sort from the bench, but Coach Crowder left him on his own. Tim called a buttonhook pass in the huddle, risky against a bunched defense, but possible if the defense believed he would not dare take the risk.

When the Mohawks came to the line, however, an overshift to the outside by one of the linebackers, caused Tim to change his mind. He called the live code letter for a signal change and selected a play that would send Joe Culler through the line into the weak spot when the Broncos were likely to expect a pass. It almost worked—not quite. The Mohawk linemen did their part. The catch was that a stunting Bronco linebacker worked himself, probably by accident, into Culler's path, made a desperate tackle, and held Culler to a four-yard gain.

So there it was—fourth down, four to go, within easy field-goal distance. Tim was certain that Coach Crowder would take action. He watched anxiously for the field-goal specialist to come onto the field, but no kicker left the bench, no replacement with instructions. The coach seemed determined to have Tim call a play that had to go at least four yards.

Tim's call was one of desperation, almost of panic. He leaned against the one strong wall he knew he could depend on. He said to Bobo, "Can you take me through?"

"Don't ask silly questions," scolded Bobo. "Here we go."

Tim spread his line, and the Broncos obediently spread their defense. Tim called his audibles, trying to put on a convincing act of selecting a good spot for his pass. When the ball was snapped, Tim crouched behind the solid bulwark of Tom Duff and Bobo. Duff's charge was good, but Bobo's was unstoppable. Tim followed Bobo's protective rear and kept on driving hard.

When he was finally smothered under a pile of sweating bodies he had no way of knowing where he was. He felt the referee's hands clawing for the ball. Tim released it grudgingly. The official pressed the ball against the ground, glanced briefly toward the side line, then swept his arm in a glorious gesture toward the goal line. First down! The Broncos yelled for a measurement, which turned out to be a waste of time. When the chain came in, the Mohawks had a yard to spare.

Tim had an intense feeling of assurance that the breaks were with him, that he had to ride his luck, and that his luck would hold. He must have communicated his attitude to the Mohawks in the huddle. They came to the line of scrimmage confident of what was in store for them.

The play broke smoothly. The Broncos put on another blitz, which the Mohawks met and crushed. Tim faked a pass to his flanker, turned his eyes and saw what he was looking for. Nick was running a sweet pattern. He sprinted diagonally and drew defenders with him. When Nick made his cut Tim released the ball, knowing where the ball would go and that Nick would be there to receive it. And that's the way the touchdown happened. Nick was near the coffin corner when the ball settled snugly in his arms. The extra point was good, and the Mohawks were back in the ball game, trailing now by only five points, 29–24.

When the defensive team took over, Tim sat reluctantly on the bench, not wanting to be out of action. Coach Crowder stopped in front of him. He did no more than grin and slap Tim lightly on the leg. It was enough.

The defensive team caught the fever the offensive team brought with it off the field. They stopped the Bronco drive, but not before the Broncos had hacked out a pair of first downs to consume time. When they were forced to kick, the runback brought the ball to the Mohawk thirty-four-yard line, and the attacking team went onto the field again.

Tim had the pleasant feeling of being among men

who trusted him, or more than that, depended on him. The feeling should have frightened him a little, but it didn't. He was convinced that he could bring the team and himself into high gear again.

He set out to prove it, but was hobbled by a series of bad breaks. No quarterback could have asked for better pass protection than the Mohawks gave him, much better than they had given the others. The team may have felt that Muller and Fisher were able to take care of themselves and that Luke did not deserve protection. It may, too, have regarded Tim as its last slim hope, someone who had to be shielded carefully to keep the game from bursting wide open.

But Tim ran into a handicap he had not anticipated. The left end, Mark Penny, a seasoned pro and a fine receiver, was not coordinating well with him. The rest of the Mohawks had managed to digest the fact that a raw rookie had gained their confidence in an incredibly short time. Mark Penny found it harder to accept. He could not believe that an inexperienced rookie could place a pass exactly where it should be placed, with the result that Mark often ruined his pass patterns by looking back too soon. Mark recognized this fact and took full blame.

During a time out Mark confessed, "I'm messing you up, Tim, and I'm sorry. Maybe I just can't believe in miracles, but I'm trying."

Mark's admission placed an extra burden on Nick

Jeffer. Of course, Mark might snap out of it at any moment, and Crowder left him in the game hoping that he would. The Mohawks, however, were running out of moments. The Broncos wisely double-teamed on Nick, which cramped the Tim-Nick combination some, but not entirely. Tim moved the Mohawks to the twenty-six-yard line before the first serious bad break. Stu Klein was hit by a pair of Bronco tacklers on an end sweep. They knocked him cold. Stu fumbled and a Bronco back recovered.

Tim squirmed miserably on the bench while the Bronco offensive team killed time deliberately. They ground out one first down. In the next series of downs a Bronco fumble bobbled crazily about the field, skittered toward the Mohawk end zone, and was recovered by the Broncos for another first down.

They stalled some more, froze the ball, and took a couple of five-yard delay of game penalties while they clung to their five-point lead. When they were finally forced to kick, and the Mohawks returned the ball to their own thrity-eight-yard line, the game was four minutes and thirty seconds from the final gun.

Tim led the Mohawks onto the field, trying not to think of the remaining time, which was so discouragingly short. He kept his mind on football, concentrating on the game with all his power. He had stored up valuable information on the Bronco defense, the strengths and weaknesses of each man who played against him. Now he used every crumb of this information. He moved the team upfield, wasting no motion, but playing deliberately, trying hard to subdue his panicky haste lest it be transmitted to the other men.

Once more he moved the team into Bronco territory, taking chances when he felt he must, avoiding reckless plays that might lose the ball and thus lose the game. No one had to tell him that this chance was the last for the Mohawks on offense. The ball was on the Bronco thirty-two-yard line, second down and six, when the official came on the field with the two-minute warning.

The defense was growing tighter as the defensive area decreased. The Broncos were desperate too. A pass to Mark Penny came within a hairbreadth of completion, but the hairbreadth might as well have been a mile. Third down and still six to go. With the defense spread against a pass, Tim was able to send Joe Culler through for the first down. It gave Tim four extra downs to use and a scant forty seconds in which to use them.

He called a sideline pass in the huddle. Once on the line he had a crazy hunch, gamble, sure, but it was time to gamble. He called the live letter in his audible, following the letter with the signal change, the first of its kind he had called today. He called his own signal for a keeper. He had not dared to try a running play before because, as the Mohawks' only remaining quarterback, he could not subject himself to the risk of injury that a running play always carries with it. At this stage of the game, however, Tim himself was easily expendable. He reasoned, too, that the advantage might be his. The Broncos had never seen him run, knew nothing of his style. So Tim called the signal, placing the Mohawks' fate in the speed of his own two legs.

The play broke fast. Tim faded toward the side line. As he cocked his arm he saw the Broncos scramble to their defensive posts. He made the passing fake, then yanked the ball down level with his waist, ready to shift it to the crook of the arm he judged safer.

The Broncos had never seen Tim run. They saw him now, moving with carefully controlled speed that he could change at will, retaining balance all the while. As he had hoped, the Broncos were caught off guard, wasting a precious instant as they stared and tried to believe their eyes.

The Mohawks were under no such handicap. Knowing in advance what to expect, they could forget about a pass and go to work on the defenders. They did a job of it. Swift, savage blocks left astounded Broncos on the field. There wasn't much for Tim to do—a few quick swivels of his hips, a change of pace, and he was in the end zone, almost disappointed he had made the trip so easily.

Tim and Nick left the field together, making way for the defensive team. Coach Crowder met them at the side line. His face was haggard from long strain, but his eyes were happy and alive.

"For a couple of green rookies," Crowder said, "you boys did fine." His voice was not too steady, when he added, "No one could have done better. Thanks, kids."

He turned away to watch the Broncos make their final futile effort. When it fizzled out, the two friends started toward the dressing room. Tim was glad to see Nick smiling in a relaxed, contented way.

Tim said, "It worked out fine. You had your big day, Nick."

"Mission accomplished," Nick agreed. "And speaking of big days, you didn't do so bad yourself. I got what I wanted, and there's no doubt that you'll get the things you want—a lot of fat Mohawk contracts that'll pay your way to fame and glory as an architect. You've made it, pal. You're in."

Tim stared blankly for a moment. "Things have been happening so fast," he said, "I haven't had time to think about that part of it." He thought about it then. Finally in a husky and uneven voice he said with wonder, "Yes, I guess I'm in."